THE ROLES WE PLAY

JON DEL ARROZ

Rislandia Books

Rachel

"Let's get these tables cleaned up and get out of here," the manager, Chris, said, clapping his hands several times as if the staff needed any motivation to go home. He stood about half a head shorter than her, slightly pudgy but not too fat, wearing a black button-down shirt and jeans as he did every night.

It was three o'clock in the morning on the Nashville strip, and the bar was finally shutting down for the night. They'd open again at ten, but at least Rachel wouldn't have to be there. She'd had a hard enough of a night, with men from a bachelor party getting extra grabby. Like usual, she sucked it up by forcing a smile, something she'd done on all too many nights. But if she wanted decent enough tips for maintaining her downtown apartment, she had to take her lumps—or let them take their lumps.

Not that she had very many. Rachel had a lithe form, and the manager clarified that she would have to stuff her bra to impress the clientele. So many little things about being here irked her, but the biggest issue was she was too bright for this. She'd gotten her degree and had a year's internship experience abroad. So why wouldn't anyone hire her?

In frustration, Rachel cleared the table too quickly, knocking over a half-empty jack and coke someone had left when the bar closed. The liquid gushed to the table's edge, ending on her dress and bare legs. It was sticky, and who knew what kind of germs the person drinking it carried? Rachel got goosebumps and wanted to wretch thinking of it.

She grabbed her rag to try to stop the flow of the mixed drink, though much of it dripped to the floor anyway. She couldn't avoid stepping in it, her heels becoming as sticky as her legs.

If only this were the first time she'd made such a spill, she might not have gotten so hot in the face, but she had an incident like this almost every night. She couldn't help it. It was too easy to get lost in thought, dreaming of something better than this nightmare of a bar.

Chris appeared beside her with a mop, quickly getting the liquid off the floor. As much as he ordered everyone around, he was hands-on and liked to help. Rachel appreciated it about him, though she wouldn't tell him. His ego was already enough.

"No need to make things so… complicated, Lavigne." He chuckled to himself as if he were the funniest person on earth.

Her last name had been the butt of jokes since she arrived. Avril. Adam. There were too many Lavignes in the music industry for her not to deal with the comments. And they were hardly anything she hadn't had to hear since junior high, especially the complicated joke.

"Ha, ha," Rachel said dryly, not in the mood.

Chris's eyes softened as he looked upon her with concern. "You've had a tough night. Why don't you bug off a little early? Jenny and I have this handled."

Jenny had a full tray, bringing it to the kitchen counter. She hollered from across the room with her deep Southern accent. "Speak for y'all's self. I got a date with Paul. He's waiting for me downstairs. I'm the one who needs to leave."

Rachel looked up at the other girl. Jenny did a better job of getting tips than her. She was bubbly, and as a blonde-haired, blue-eyed, all-American, the people who came to get the Nashville experience were looking for someone just like her. They wore the same cocktail dress, but while Rachel looked awkward with her height, Jenny came across as an elegant southern belle ready for the ball. Nevertheless, she couldn't help but feel jealous sometimes.

"It's fine," Rachel said. "I've got nothing to do."

"I don't want you to burn out," Chris said.

"I said it's fine." But, unfortunately, she came across as terser than she intended. Maybe those bachelors had gotten to her more than she realized, or perhaps the job had her down. Either way, Rachel was miserable and burned out. But she wouldn't complain. She needed this job. It paid decently enough to where she could survive. What more could she ask for?

Jenny had set down her things and picked up her handbag—a Cristin Loubitton piece way more expensive than her waitressing job should have been able to afford. Where had she gotten that?

"Bless your heart, love." Jenny got up on her tiptoes and kissed Rachel on the cheek. Her eyes were bright and sparkling, and when Rachel looked to the end of the bar, she could see why.

A man leaned against the bartop. Dark, handsome, wearing a shirt with the top button undone to show off his chest. He looked like a dream—a dream Rachel would never find.

Jenny swayed her hips over to him, laying it on thick. It made Rachel want to roll her eyes, but the man at the end of the bar stared at her, completely fixated. How did the other girls play such games? Ugh.

Rachel gave one last look back. "Rach, Chris, meet Paul, my new boyfriend. He's a sweetie."

"'Sup," the dark, handsome man said.

Rachel had her hands full but tried to force a smile anyway. "Nice to meet you."

"You take care of her," Chris said, sounding as if he were a brother or a father. He was sweet in his own way, but even he had a wife and kids at home. Rachel sometimes felt like she was the only single person left in Nashville.

"Oh, I will," Paul said.

Jenny linked arms with him, and they turned and left.

Without the help of Jenny, it took another thirty minutes to clean up the place, but they'd finally gotten it done. It wasn't the worst night, but not the best either, and tomorrow they'd start it all over again.

Rachel clocked out, giving Chris a wave and friendly goodbye on her way, putting on a coat and her backpack before heading out. She called an Uber, not about to bring a car downtown to work, and try to navigate the nightmare of parking.

She nearly fell asleep on the ride home before talking up the creaking stairs to the second floor of an older apartment off H Street. Not the best neighborhood, but she didn't feel like she was about to be attacked either.

Her apartment was small, a studio with a little kitchenette, a bed that took up too much room, and a modest bathroom with a shower. What she wouldn't have given to have a bathtub to soak in at night like this. She didn't have a TV, never needing anything beyond her laptop, which she had on a small desk in the corner.

She flopped down on the bed face-first, still in her work clothes. Immediately, she regretted that decision, as she had to have had all the germs of the city on her, which she now transferred to her comforter. What was she thinking?

Rachel was too tired to think. But she picked herself up anyway and hopped into the shower, spending far too long there as well. By the time she'd finished, it was close to five in the morning, but the shower left Rachel wired. She couldn't sleep.

Now in soft sweatpants and a hoodie, Rachel opened her laptop. Nothing looked good on YouTube or Netflix, not that she thought anything would. She immediately turned to her addiction that no one knew about and opened her chat program.

One thing she didn't talk about in the bar was her love of science fiction. Despite it becoming somewhat more acceptable to be a geek girl in recent years, she felt like a pretender with her fandom. She'd never wanted to be a cosplayer like she'd seen many other girls who shared her interests do. It was too exhibitionist. All she wanted to do was read. She loved the classics—Heinlein, Anderson, Asprin, Pournelle. However, something about space marines gave her goosebumps. Not that she wanted to be one, but more that she wanted one. It was a stupid fantasy, making her laugh in her apartment. Of course, none of it was real, but she couldn't help what she found attractive.

She'd found this chat room by accident a few months ago, with almost a hundred people playing characters in what they called The Aryshan Wars universe, based on a novel series of the same name. It had many options for cool alien species, built-in conflict, and the perfect role-playing setting.

And she'd fallen in love with it, creating her character, Veela, the Eternite.

Space Adventures Online

#General

▭

Veela: What's up guys?
  Lizyin (GM): Hey Veela
  Lt. Chandler: Yo.
  Veela: I can't believe I'm still awake. My stupid work has me thinking too much to sleep.
  Lizyin (GM): What's it there? 4:00?
  Veela: 5
  Lizyin (GM): Crazy. It's 11 A.M. over here. Ready to go.
  Veela: Anything fun going on?
  Lizyin (GM): I was about to start an adventure open to anyone, but most of the Americans aren't on right now. You want me to run you an adventure?
  Veela: My fav GM :)
  Lt. Chandler: Can I play?

Lizyin (GM): Sure. Need a few more people, to be honest.

Veela: We could get Ray or Aria if we wait a few hours. Everyone else is using the alternate server for the bigger space battle plot between Earth and Arysha.

Lizyin (GM): Do you want to wait?

Veela: lol not really.

Lizyin (GM): Okay then. Hop into #Palmer-Station and post your intros.

#Palmer-Station

Lizyin (GM): Palmer Station is a large station, a port of call toward the border of Earth's domain, intersecting perfectly where the Drenite and Aryshans can utilize it as a trade hub. Because of the big-three's use, the smaller planetary empires use it as well. There's opportunity, but there's also danger because of so many different interests gathered together. You exit onto the spaceport floor, gathering with thousands.

Veela: Veela exited her transport, glancing around wide-eyed. It had been her first time off of the Eternite homeworld, at least in this form. She recalled her past lives, a part of her yet still separate. One had been a pilot, but that was a long time ago. She wore a black jumpsuit, dark colors helping her to blend in. She wanted adventure, but more, she wanted to make it as a successful freighter captain. She had her ship, now all she needed was a crew and a mission.

Lt. Chandler: Chandler, an officer in the Interplanetary Navy, watched as the newcomers came aboard. He worked security for the station, standing in his grays, his rank stripes displayed on his right breast. He noticed Veela. "What's your business on the station?"

Veela: "Looking for work." Veela gave him a bright smile. It tended to disarm men most of the time.

Lt. Chandler: This time was no different. She was pretty, her alien features making her all the more exotic to Chandler. "Do you require an escort?"

Veela: "Is the station a dangerous place?"

Lt. Chandler: He grinned. "Not with security like me around. Where are you headed?"

Lizyin (GM): You would hear there is a representative of the Archeological Guild named Jorin Issim looking for explorers. He's located in the Green Sector.

Veela: "The Archeological Guild. Jorin Issim — are you familiar?"

Lt. Chandler: "Hmm, Green Sector. That's a hodge-podge of alien representatives. Difficult to navigate."

Veela: Her smile brightened, eyes shining at the lieutenant. "No trouble for security like you, right?'

Lt. Chandler: "Nope. Follow me." He led her to Green Sector, navigating through the crowds of people.

Ray Athan: ((is it too late to join?))

Lizyin (GM): ((not at all, just getting started))

Ray Athan: Ray stood in dark clothing, shades concealing his eyes, scanning the crowd. The rogue had concealed weapons he didn't much want security to find, and was hungry for action. He spotted Veela and she looked like she'd be a good mark.

Lizyin (GM): They all proceeded into Green Sector without incident where they entered a strange alien tea shop with a curtain covering the front. Pushing it aside, there were all sorts of strange aromas from cinnamon to cow dung—aliens had a wide array of tastes. It all mixed together in the air in a smoky atmosphere.

Veela: She scrunched her nose as she entered. "Gross."

Lt. Chandler: "This is why I stay out of Green Sector, generally." He followed her.

Jorin Issim (NPC): The Aryshan man of the Akkad (Worker) tribe sat in the corner, engaged in business negotiations. They ended quickly and he returned to sipping a strange orange brew of tea. He seemed approachable enough.

Veela: She motioned Chandler to join her. "Here goes."

$$\rule{3cm}{0.4pt}$$

Jason

$$\rule{3cm}{0.4pt}$$

Five-Thirty A.M., and Jason was wired from his Kick Ass Coffee, which allegedly had double the caffeine of regular brews. He'd grown addicted a long time ago, needing it to get up in time for the markets to open in New York and make his morning trades.

He sat with a laptop on his lap in his favorite leather chair, reclining in the open living room attached to the kitchen. Only a countertop separated them, like a bar he could walk around, and both rooms had floor-to-ceiling windows looking out upon his deck and his Nevada ranch outside.

It was a beautiful house, forty-five hundred square feet of elegance. The house had everything he could ever want and at a third of the price of a tiny shack in Orange County, where he'd grown up. It had been the right move, and he could work the markets from anywhere, so why not?

The only problem was that it felt so empty with a house of such a size. His cleaners would arrive in a couple of hours, with his personal trainer an hour later, but they were just temporary guests. It wasn't as if he didn't have any friends, but there were only so many people he could handle, and he'd kept many of those relationships at arm's length since the split with Danielle.

He didn't want to think about her, but the quiet of the mornings bothered him more than he wanted to let on. He needed something to do to occupy his mind.

Until recently, he'd been playing the **MMORPG** World of Warriors, a fantasy game that had hit the spot for the last couple of years. He'd joined one of the best raiding guilds on the server as a barbarian, his damage off the charts, but there was something repetitive in boring in grinding for gold and gear over and over. Even though the game designers had done their best to design the dungeons differently, Jason got bored.

He ran a hand through his black hair, which seemed to fall into place without much effort. He usually received compliments on his hair and smile, but even getting those had started to feel empty lately.

What could he do? He could go on vacation, but he'd be in the same rut, just waking up somewhere else to log onto the markets, go out to restaurants, walk around, go to bars, go to sleep, and repeat. Doing so somewhere like Barcelona, with a whole city of dark-haired Spanish beauties around could be a lot more fun than Reno, but he burned out of partying as quickly as he'd burned out of work.

Working was just a habit for him at this point. He'd made millions on the markets. Even if it tanked, he had enough assets now to where he'd be set for life, but there was a thrill in getting things done and winning that kept him going. He supposed it was a lot like why he still played World of Warriors.

But he wanted something different.

Jason pulled up a new tab on his browser and considered what he wanted. Not a new YouTube or Netflix show. Those had bored him to tears lately. Nothing gave him the rush World of Warriors used to in the beginning.

He typed new RPG into the search bar and hit send. The tab populated with dozens of links. More video games that were clones of World of Warriors popped up. He didn't want those either. But for some reason, he felt compelled to continue to pages two and three of the search results.

There, he found something different. Space Adventures Online. Was this a sci-fi game? He clicked on it.

The website didn't look very professional, like someone had taken a basic template and placed a few images on it. Not the work of a good video game company.

But as he read, he saw this wasn't a video game. Text chatroom roleplaying? Odd. It sounded like something dated from the early days of the internet, but it had a button on the page that read "click here to enter." So he figured he'd give it a whirl and try it out.

Space Adventures Online

———————————

#General

———

Lizyin: Welcome @Jas868!

Lt. Chandler: Welcome!

Jas868: Hey. Just checking things out.

Lizyin (GM):Let us know if you have any questions. You can work on your character on the template here. #Character-Template

Jas868: I'm not even sure what this is.

Ray Athan: This is a text roleplaying game based on the Aryshan Wars novel series. Most of the action takes place aboard Palmer Station where aliens gather as a commerce hub to trade, dispense missions, etc.

Lizyin (GM): Think of it as a collaborative writing experience. We all make our own characters and play out scenarios through creative text writing. In a lot of ways it's like writing our own book set in the universe, but it's kind of different since you need to respect what the other players decide. It's really fun. We're live right now you can watch in the #Palmer-Station channel.

Jas868: Alright, I think I'll watch for a while. Sounds good.

#Palmer-Station

Jorin Issim (NPC): Jorin looked up at the people approaching him. "Can I help you?"

Veela: Veela glanced at Chandler before smiling at the Aryshan. "Yes. I'm looking for work and heard you might be able to help u.s"

Jorin Issim (NPC): "Depends on who you are." He raised a curious brow at them.

Lt. Chandler: I'm Lt. Chandler, station security.

Jorin Issim (NPC): Jorin laughed. "This isn't the place for security."

Lt. Chandler: "I like credits. Having a side gig isn't a bad thing."

Veela: "That's right. And I'm Captain Veela of the freighter ship *Sunflower*.

Jorin Issim (NPC): "Sunflower?"

Veela: "As pretty as she sounds." Veela smiled proudly about her ship. "Now what have you got? We're ready to go."

Ray Athan: Ray continued to watch and listen quietly from his corner.

Jorin Issim (NPC): "Well then, captain. I have a client who is seeking the Orb of Reckoning, an ancient artifact of the Kraleen people, a race long dead, or at least having abandoned their homeworld. The Orb is said to be contained in the depths of the Ruins of Aethon. No one's been able to retrieve it for me so far. My client will pay handsomely if you are able."

Veela: Veela considered. The Orb sounded interesting enough. But if someone was willing to pay so much, there must be more to the story. Still, it wasn't her business to question. She had a job to do. "We'll take it, but I want trip expenses covered."

Jorin Issim (NPC): "Only if you find the orb and return with it. The Archeological Guild has government funding, but it's not unlimited. We have to have something to show for our efforts that's valuable for science or historical pursuits or we won't be able to get the funding to pay you."

Lt. Chandler: "Sounds sketchy. Maybe we should find a stabler job. We can't eat 'maybes', after all."

Veela: She was determined, narrowing her eyes at Chandler. The guild would pay handsomely if they succeeded? They operated in a business of big risks and big reward, and she wanted to take it. "No. We're in."

Jorin Issim (NPC): He grinned. "Very well. I wish you luck. Now leave me to enjoy my drink."

Veela: Veela nodded and started to walk away.

Ray Athan: Ray signaled for Veela to come over to him. He had a vaporless nicotine stick in his hand, glowing whenever he took a puff.

Veela: She stopped her exit and made her way to Ray. "Yes?"

Ray Athan: "Ray Athan. I heard you're going on an assignment around the Kraleen system. I happen to have traveled there several times during my training years. I can probably show you around, for a price. I'm a good pilot and better company."

Veela: She glanced at Chandler.

Lt. Chandler: "We don't need his type on our mission. He'll probably steal the orb and run off with it."

Ray Athan: "Where would I go? I'd be stuck out in space and needing your ship for transport."

Veela: "We're not afraid. What's your price?"

Ray Athan: "Six hundred credits."

Veela: "You're crazy."

Ray Athan: "I'm worth it." He gave her a bright smile.

Veela: "You'd better be. I need crew, though, so you've got a deal. Come meet us in Docking Bay Twenty Two."

Ray Athan: "I'll see you there."

Veela: She walked out with Chandler.

2

Jason

Jason watched the text unfold before him. It looked like a lot of fun. These people made their own characters, not from some template where you could choose between a couple of different hairstyles for aesthetics, but truly created their own characters. They were like real people with jobs, lives, friends… lovers?

How far did this go anyway? Did people play out relationships on this thing? He didn't see anyone flirting in the scene, but trying was a little tempting.

His head filled with the image of someone suave, though not too unlike himself, to go in and be calm. This Veela person would take notice. That could be fun.

Jason smiled to himself.

He was already getting caught up in the whole scene, and he hadn't even played yet. But the idea spurred his imagination. It wouldn't just be fun but something he could be creative with.

A timer went off, reminding Jason to make his mid-day plays on the markets. He had to return to work, but the chat role-play was all he could think about. His character couldn't be one of those incredible alien races from the novels. He didn't know enough about it and would feel like a pretender going through there.

Instead of checking the stocks, he visited fan sites to learn more about the books. The Aryshans, a proud alien race who shared empathic bonds with one another in tribes. How interesting. He could only imagine being able to sense someone's emotions in real life. It would make things easier, knowing where people stood. So much of human interaction involved guesswork, and if you guessed wrong…

…well, it ended up with a situation with his ex, Danielle. She was beautiful, so much he got caught up in her, but she only cared about herself. Everything was her problem. He had to dote on her. He had to buy her things. But she never paid attention to him when it came down to it.

Classic narcissism, his brother had told him at the time. But when Jason fell, he didn't fall easy. He had blinders on the entire way regarding her.

In the end, however, Jason had been the one to torpedo the relationship. For all of her faults, she hadn't actually wronged her. He bore the guilt of their split.

His shoulders tightened at the thought, and he found himself pounding out the keys on his keyboard when trying to make his stock trades. It made his wrists sore. He couldn't think about her. They'd called off their engagement. It was over. This was precisely why he needed stress relief to get his mind off his life.

It was hard enough as it was, to have a life. Doing investments and trading meant everything could be handled online. He used a few trader websites and mostly communicated through email. He still had his one wealthy client from Irvine, Jesus Rodriguez, who called him occasionally, but Jason could live his entire life alone in his big house, and few would notice his disappearance.

Sure, he had to call his family occasionally, but it felt like an obligation, not being social. So how had his life gotten to this point?

He shook his head. Work had to be the focus for now. Then he could play. And what he wanted to play was Space Adventures Online.

Space Adventures Online

#General

Jas868: I really need a new chat name. This doesn't fit in thematically.

Lizyin (GM): When you make your character you can change your username by using /nick and then the name afterward.

Jas868: Cool.

Veela: You thinking of a character? We could use more for our "Indiana Jones In Space!" mission.

Ray Athan: Lol. That's totally what it is, isn't it?

Veela: Yeah.

Jas868: I think I'll just make a human cuz I don't know the setting all that well. I don't want to mess anything up.

Veela: Most everyone is pretty chill and will help you. If you want to play an alien, go for it. I did, and an obscure one at that.

Jas868: I'm okay with human. Thanks though.

Aria Benoit: Hey everyone.

Lt. Chandler: Hello, Aria. Been awhile.

Aria Benoit: I've been busy with exams. What'd I miss?

Lt. Chandler: We're starting up a new mission.

Aria Benoit: Ah. Let me know if you need a cybernetic ally enhanced engineer/hacker.

Veela: Come join the Sunflower. We can chat.

Aria Benoit: Where to?

Veela: #Sunflower of course. Lol

Aria Benoit: Ok.

Jas868: Would I be able to make a character for the Sunflower too?

Veela: I don't see why not.

Jas868: Cool. What do you need?

Lt. Chandler: I've got security handled. Ray Athan is piloting, and Aria plays one of the best engineers out there.

Veela: Hmm…

Lizyin (GM): Do you guys have a medic?

Veela: Oh! No, we don't. That would work great.

Jas868: Huh. I hadn't thought about a doctor as a character. I guess I can do that.

Lizyin (GM): No pressure. Play what you want to play.

Jas868: It's a good idea. A mercenary doctor. Sounds fun.

Lizyin (GM): Don't forget to look at the bio sheet, fill it out completely. If you have any questions we're here.

Jas868: Cool Thanks.

Bio Sheet

Character Bio:

Name: Dr. Donovan Conley
    Age: 27
    Species/Race: Human
    Nickname/Alias: Don
    Gender: Male
    Department: Medical - Mercenary
    Rank: N/A
    Position: N/A
    Applicable Training:
    - Medical Ethics
    - Pediatric Medicine
    - Xeno Biology
    - Field Medicine

Appearance: Don stood at 6'0", athletic in his build from running in and out of different tense situations as a field medic for mercenary groups.

Character Biography & Background: Don grew up on Earth with two parents. He was a relation to the famous Admiral Conley as a nephew, his father deciding not to go into fleet but stay in business with banking back on Earth.

Don was always the type to have a compassionate heart growing up, sensitive about wounded animals, wanting to fix a problem whenever he saw a kid hurt on the playground. That fascination stayed with him as he grew up.

He was accepted into Nevada St. University where he got a degree in biology, a fan of their football team. He joined a fraternity of other pre-med students and had a good time in college before graduating.

He then went to med school at NYU, a big culture shock from Nevada in the busy New York area. But with med school being so all-consuming, he barely got to explore the area. He never went out, focused.

From there, he had his residency on the Lunar Colony, his first time off planet, an interesting experience as he tended to people from the Interplanetary Navy or other Space Traders. It was fun hearing of far off worlds. He also encountered his first live Aryshan and Tralos, learning about the different physiologies as they came into the ICU.

Once his residency was over, a trader captain approached him for a stint going back and forth from the Cestus colony, hearing about various different ports out there. It was an easy assignment within human space, controlled by Earth and the Interplanetary Navy.

The assignment ended, and he came to Palmer Station to look for work.

Other information:
　　Likes: Helping others, Friends, Coffee
　　Dislikes: Bullies, Selfishness, Getting too close to airlocks
　　Timezone: EST

Rachel

The next day of work went by terribly slowly for Rachel. The Nashville strip sounded great when she'd first come to town, but after a while, it became stale. During the week, the same bands played their exact same sets. If she had to hear Journey's Don't Stop Believin' with a country twang twist one more time, she would claw someone's eyes out.

The only thing that kept her from going crazy was her roleplaying chat. While the songs blared, the drunks stumbled, and the fry cooks screwed up simple orders of chicken tenders—which she never could figure out how they managed to do—Rachel could lose herself in thoughts of a different world light years away.

It'd taken months for her to get to the point where she could captain her own ship. She'd worked her way up the ranks. Even though she technically was a civilian outfit, the GMs didn't let just anyone have their own ship. It was a privilege for good roleplay and hard work in the game. She'd finally gotten there.

The thought of a crew ready and willing to follow her gave her goosebumps. With Paul here, she'd never even make manager in her real life, let alone command some kind of ship.

Her thoughts of her game and planning for the Sunflower's adventures kept her going throughout the day. Nothing could faze her. The whole shift seemed to pass in a whirlwind.

When it ended, she said her goodbyes, not paying any particular note to what any of her coworkers said before heading to the back parking lot. Even though she could log on and type with a full keyboard when she got home, Rachel couldn't help but check the chat from her phone. She was too excited.

Before too long, she was back in her apartment again. She barely remembered talking to Chris, Jenny, or the bartender, Bill. Where had the night gone?

These made for the best kinds of evenings, though.

Maybe it was stupid for her to be happy because of some people online. If she told anyone at work she spent her days playing Space Adventures Online, they'd look at her like she was crazy. Her friends back home would think the same. Rachel laughed as she thought about how absurd her life had become.

But despite having gone to Vanderbilt, her five years in Nashville hadn't made the place feel like a home. After college, when so many people left—like her roommate Sammy back to Michigan— she lost a lot of friends. It was too draining to go out and make a bunch of new ones, at least in person.

In all that amount of time, this still didn't feel like home.

It wasn't like she could return to her family's place in South Carolina. Her dad would never understand how she spent four years working hard to get her degree and could not get a job beyond being a waitress in a honky tonk bar.

It was embarrassing. She had student loans mounting, and all it would result in would be an uncomfortable lecture about how in his day, he'd "walked right into an office and said he'd prove his worth to the firm." Life didn't work like that anymore. It hadn't in decades.

South Carolina couldn't be her home any more than Nashville.

Rachel sighed, not wanting to think about everything, get stressed out, and spiral into something worse. The last time she'd done that, she'd cried her eyes out for two days straight, missing work. She couldn't afford to do that now.

She opened her laptop, the screen's glow making her wince as her eyes adjusted to the bright light. A lot of the time, she didn't remember to actually turn on her apartment lights, sitting in the dark to stare at her computer.

The chatroom page loaded, still open from the night before, automatically logging her in with her saved information. Rachel stretched out her fingers and readied herself for another night of roleplay.

But it looked like she had a DM from someone she had to answer first.

Space Adventures Online

#DM-Dr.-Donovan-Conley

Dr. Donovan Conley: Hey

Veela: Hello?

Dr. Donovan Conley: Oh, sorry. This is Jas868. I got my nickname changed.

Veela: Ah. Hey. I didn't know they allowed characters with canon names.

Dr. Donovan Conley: I couldn't come with a name so I thought it'd be easiest to make a character related to one on the wiki sheet.

Veela: Well, Conley's a big character in the series. Not Donovan, though. Matthew. He's an admiral who won the Drenite War and was a big thorn in the Aryshan fleet's side in the main trilogy. It's rumored he's going to have a son who's the main character of the next installment.

Dr. Donovan Conley: Yeah, Don would be the admiral's nephew. Hope that's not too canon?

Veela: If Lizyin says it's good, then we oblige by her rulings. She's the Game Master, so her word is law.

Dr. Donovan Conley: Nice. She told me it'd be fine, but to not have Donovan too close to the canon characters, that way he can be independent. I've got the character all ready. I was hoping we could play and meet about the mission thing?

Veela: We can do that.

Dr. Donovan Conley: Alright, bear with me. I haven't played before. Don't know what I'm doing.

Veela: You'll be fine. Have fun.

#Sunflower

Veela: The Sunflower was docked in Palmer Station's Bay Twenty-Two with several crates of cargo outside. It was a modest sized ship, three levels. A cockpit/bridge and mess hall up top, an engine room and cargo bays down below. The crew quarters were on the second deck, along with a rec room for working out and having fun and a medical facility. The ramp was descended from the rear cargo bay to allow entry.

Dr. Donovan Conley: Don made his way to the ship, looking at it. It was smaller than his last assignment, but he didn't have fancy needs. He had his bag of medical supplies with him in his left hand as he walked in.

Veela: The captain stood in the cargo bay, checking on rations an provisions for the next leg of their journey to make sure they were well-stocked.

Dr. Donovan Conley: He stepped inside the bay. "Hello?"

Veela: Veela turned around, her white hair flowing halfway down her back. The Eternites looked much like humans, excepting silver eyes which had no contrast between pupils or otherwise. Those orbs focused on him. "Hello. You must be the new doctor?"

Dr. Donovan Conley: Don did his best to smile, hoping he didn't come across as too nervous for the job assignment. Despite having a few trips around different planets under his belt, he'd never met Eternites before. Her eyes fascinated him. "Yes. Donovan Conley. You can call me Don."

Veela: Her lips ticked up into a small grin. "Are you sure you don't want to be called doctor? I find most medical professionals I met prefer the title."

Dr. Donovan Conley: "I've never been one for formalities."

Veela: "Well, I am. You'll call me captain and say yes ma'am while aboard." *She spun, her hair flowing as she walked toward the cargo bay.

Dr. Donovan Conley: He chuckled. "Yes, ma'am."

Veela: "This is our cargo bay, one of two. Your actual office will be up on the elevator, if you should choose to accept this mission."

Dr. Donovan Conley: "Choose to accept? I thought you were interviewing me." He followed along with her.

Veela: "We don't have a lot of choices if we want to leave in a timely manner. I've seen your resume. You can mend me if I get hit by a plasma burst, yes?"

Dr. Donovan Conley: "Depends on how severe it is."

Veela: She huffed. "Good answer. I'd rather you be honest with me than lie to sound good. Let me show you the way upstairs."

━━

#General

Dr. Donovan Conley: This is really fun.

Lizyin (GM): I'm glad you like it.

Veela: Happy you're enjoying yourself.

Dr. Donovan Conley: I hope I'm doing okay. This is my first time.

Veela: You actually write really well.

Dr. Donovan Conley: Thanks. You too.

Dr. Donovan Conley: Where's the rest of the crew?

Veela: Not online right now. That's the struggle. Sometimes you just gotta post and wait a few hours for someone to respond.

Dr. Donovan Conley: Ahh. I'm not the most patient.

Veela: You learn it with this game.

Lizyin (GM): Ain't that the truth.

3

Jason

Jason looked at the time at the top right corner of his laptop screen. He'd been playing for three hours! How had that even happened? It didn't feel like he'd accomplished that much, getting a tour of the ship and settling into his quarters. It was just a basic starting point, and he wanted more.

Veela was cute too. He couldn't believe he'd had the thought, but she had a little avatar icon of her character drawn, and whoever made it made her character very pretty. He'd associated the name with the picture in his mind. Crazy how this worked.

He'd never had similar thoughts with World of Warriors. Sure, a lot of people chose good-looking toons to play, but it wasn't as if they self-identified with them. Instead, there was a level of creativity in the writing, making connecting the player and character much easier. It was more intimate.

When Jason got into something, he didn't do it in half measures. He either had an intense interest or not at all. Right after logging off, he went on Amazon and ordered himself the books for the complete Aryshan Wars. Maybe it was silly to get himself several books sight unseen, but he'd enjoyed playing it enough that he already knew he liked the setting.

The books would be here in the next couple of days. Jason could have gotten ebooks, he supposed, being as impatient as he tended to be when something excited him, but as he had already stared at a computer monitor all day, he didn't like reading on a device.

The doorbell rang, interrupting his thoughts.

Jason shuffled out of his chair. It was already eleven o'clock. His personal trainer would be here. He hustled to the door to open it.

At the door stood a man one wouldn't have expected would be a personal trainer. He wasn't particularly fit, let alone buff, with a slight beer belly and nerdy-looking glasses. But at the same time, he was very attentive, knew his exercises, and most importantly, gave Jason a meal plan, making it easy for him to have a decent diet to keep up his physique. At the end of the day, Jason paid him for his own looks, not for how his trainer maintained a particular form.

"Hey, Tim," Jason said.

Tim smiled back at him. "What's going on?"

"You wouldn't believe it," Jason said. He felt embarrassed to be playing the online roleplaying game. Why? He didn't need to impress anybody, let alone Tim. His trainer loved to gab about the most recent superhero streaming shows while Jason pumped weight. He was a nerd and would understand, surely.

Tim clasped a hand on Jason's shoulder. "You still need to get into gym clothes, buddy. Tell me all about it in your weight room."

After changing, Jason stepped into his makeshift weight room. But, of course, it was a little more than makeshift, sparing no expense for top-of-the-line equipment. His job paid well, so why wouldn't he? With a Peloton bike, a treadmill, a complete set of barbells with a couple of different benches, machines, and a pull-up bar, Jason had about everything he needed in what would have been a spare bedroom for someone with a family.

It irked him sometimes, not having one, but he'd had a busy life and never wanted to pursue a serious relationship since the situation with his ex.

"You seem a little more energetic than normal," Tim said while Jason started his warm-up cardio routine to get the blood flowing.

"I'm excited," he said. The routine made him breathe a little heavier than usual, but he could still maintain a conversation. It would be the heavy weights later where Tim would keep talking, and Jason wouldn't be able to reply.

"What about?"

"It's stupid," Jason said, the twist of embarrassment making him coy about the whole thing. "I found this online roleplaying game based on some science fiction novels, and it's really cool."

"Good graphics?" Tim asked as he was familiar with Jason's World of Warriors habits.

Jason shook his head, increasing the speed on his treadmill from a walk to a jog. "No graphics at all. It's a text thing."

"Like D&D?" Tim leaned on the side of the machine.

"Kind of. They have someone storytelling and doing adventures, but it's all writing. There's no rolling or anything like that."

"Sounds cool."

"It is. I've only played once, but it gets the creative juices flowing. A nice contrast to playing the markets."

"Left and right brain," Tim agreed.

They talked about life as his routine continued.

Jason moved on to stretches and weights. Today would be leg day—which he'd seen on workout forums and comments online most people hated, but it never bothered him. Legs seemed easier than other exercise regimens, with squats, lunges, and weights to supplement. After about an hour and a half of training, he finally finished, ready to call it.

All he wanted was to get back on his game.

"Have fun with your nerd game," Tim teased with a grin as they left the weight room to head to the door.

"You have no room to talk with your Wuxia novels you keep blathering about," Jason said.

"Hey, those are cool. And they're Chinese. I'm a cultured man," Tim said.

The two clasped hands, and Tim was out the door, leaving Jason alone.

The big house seemed extra quiet when people left, giving Jason a sense of aloneness that never sat right with him. He was out of breath from the strenuous workout, sweat starting to dry on his clothes and hair.

As much as he wanted to log back online and check the chat, he desperately needed to shower, and there would be a couple more hours of work after that. He went to his kitchen to grab a protein shake out of the fridge and down it, knowing his obsessive tendencies would make this role-playing thing go overboard.

Space Adventures Online

#Sunflower

▭

Dr. Donovan Conley: Don put his supplies away in the small medical bay in the ship. It was a quaint space, but he liked it well enough.

Lt. Chandler: He walked into the medical bay. "Is this where I report for my physical?"

Dr. Donovan Conley: "I didn't know we were doing physicals." He looked up at the new arrival.

Lt. Chandler: He shrugged. "Captain's orders. Wants to make sure we're in good condition."

Dr. Donovan Conley: "Well, sit down, lift your shirt so I can listen to your heart." He picked up his stethoscope putting it into his ears.

Dr. Donovan Conley: ((Do they still use stethoscopes in this era?))

Lt. Chandler: ((I'd think we'd have electronic scanners or something. I don't really know.))

Dr. Donovan Conley: ((Well, I guess my guy will have one anyway, be old school))

Lt. Chandler: ((sounds good)

Lt. Chandler: He sat on the medical bed as directed and took his shirt off. He was muscular, with a tattoo of an eagle on his right breast.

Dr. Donovan Conley: He noted the tattoo but didn't say anything, not wanting to pry into people's private matters. He placed the stethoscope against him and listened to his heart. "Sounds good so far, and you appear in fit condition."

Lt. Chandler: "Have to be in my profession."

Dr. Donovan Conley: "And what's that?"

Lt. Chandler: "Security."

Dr. Donovan Conley: "Ah." He stepped back and grabbed an instrument to check blood pressure. It flashed with several lights as he simply placed it against the man's arm and then it produced its readings. "All looks good here as well. Any medical conditions I should be aware of?"

Lt. Chandler: "Nope."

Dr. Donovan Conley: He placed another machine on the man's skull, which also blinked with several lights. It brought up several different readings over on the computer system which Donovan then went over carefully.

Lt. Chandler: Chandler sat still, like a good security guard.

Dr. Donovan Conley: The man didn't seem to talk much, but it was fine with him. It made it easy to do the quiet work. Eventually, he moved from the computer terminal and turned back to Chandler. "I give you a clean bill of health. Do you know when we depart?"

Lt. Chandler: "As soon as the captain gets back." He put his shirt back on. "If that's all…"

Dr. Donovan Conley: He motioned for the man to go. "Nice meeting you. Don't think I caught your name."

Lt. Chandler: "Chandler."

Dr. Donovan Conley: "Don, nice to meet you."

Lt. Chandler: "See you around the ship, doc." He headed out.

#General

Dr. Donovan Conley: Cool. Wasn't expecting that.

Lt. Chandler: What?

Dr. Donovan Conley: Doing medical stuff like physicals. Didn't think of it. Funny because I decided to play a doctor.

Lt. Chandler: Pretty standard.

Dr. Donovan Conley: When do we get going though? The ship departing, I mean.

Lt Chandler: Whenever Veela's on.

Dr. Donovan Conley: Where is she?

Ray Athan: She works afternoons/evenings most of the time so she keeps hours more in line with the Euro players.

Dr. Donovan Conley: Ah. I'm up pretty early myself.

Ray Athan: Should get to play a lot then.

Dr. Donovan Conley: Cool. :)

#DM-Veela

Dr. Donovan Conley: Hey. Got going aboard the ship. I'm excited. Thanks for letting me play.

Dr. Donovan Conley: Heard you're at work. Hope all's well. Talk to you soon.

Rachel

Rachel went to her car on her lunch break with chicken tenders and tots in a tray. It wasn't her ideal meal, but the bar comped her free food while working, so she wouldn't turn it down. She had to save every penny she could.

Her phone buzzed in her purse, and Rachel scrambled in the driver's seat to get to it. Her fingers had grease from the food, but she wouldn't have time to get it off before answering. She hated touching her phone like this, but sometimes it was a necessary evil.

The screen displayed "Home." It had to be mom.

Her mother called her about three times a week, keeping in touch reasonably well. She swiped to start the call.

"Hi, Mom," Rachel said, pressing the phone to her ear and pinning it to her shoulder so she could resume eating. She only had half an hour and had to get in her meal when she could.

"It's not your mother," a distinctly male, deep voice said over the phone, slow-speaking in a southern drawl.

"Dad!" He rarely called her. It made her a little nervous. "Is everything okay?"

"Everything's fine. How is Nashville?"

"It's great." It felt like a lie when she said it. She didn't hate her life or her time here, but great was an overstatement.

"You don't sound convincing."

He called her on her bluff. She could never lie to him. Rachel had been daddy's girl growing up, but as of late, she'd felt like she was more of a disappointment to him than anything else. But, of course, this didn't help matters.

"It is. I'm working, paying off my debts." *She slinked down in the seat of her car, feeling small all of a sudden.

"Hardly working," Dad grumbled. "Listen, Mom, and I are getting worried about you. You seem like you're hardly there whenever we're talking to you. She's worried. I'm worried."

"You don't have to be. I'm fine." Rachel sounded defensive, even to herself. Was she fine? The accusation rattled her. Her days had been a blur, one after another. The same thing day in and day out, feeling like her life had little progress. And she was alone.

"You can't continue living as a young woman in some ratty apartment in a big city. It's not healthy. You're killing yourself."

Silence hung in the car for a long moment, Rachel trying to keep it together. Why did he have to do this now? "Dad..."

"No, listen. Mom and I have discussed this. We know you have student loans and are struggling, so here's what we suggest—you move back in with us for a while, get things sorted out, look for a real job, and we'll cover your debts for the time being. First, you have to get out of that environment."

"Dad, I can't. I'm doing this on my own." She started to choke up. She couldn't do this and go back to work. Her fingernails dug into the edge of the driver's seat, knuckles turning white.

"Yes, you can. I'm trying to help, Rach. Don't—"

Rachel couldn't take it anymore. She hung up the phone.

Space Adventures Online

#Sunflower

▭

Veela: She walked onto the bridge of her ship, glancing at the stations there. "Status Report."

Ray Athan: He tapped his station. "About ready to enter the system."

Lt. Chandler: "Weapons online. Shields at maximum."

Veela: "Then we won't have any surprises." Veela nodded as she stood in front of the captain's chair.

Dr. Donovan Conley: He stood at the back of the bridge, observing the crew. He wouldn't be needed until a medical emergency, but he would be there and ready when the time was right.

Veela: Out of the corner of her eye, he saw Dr. Conley, noting the doctor's professional patience.

Dr. Donovan Conley: He gave Veela a small smile.

Veela; Veela returned the smile.

Lizyin (GM): When you enter the system, all seems

quiet. The world is green and peaceful, looking like no one had been there for a thousand years, but then several projectiles come your way!

Lt. Chandler: "Missiles incoming!"

Veela: "See if you can shoot them down." Veela took her seat and braced herself for impact.

Lt. Chandler: He used the targeting computer to attempt to shoot the missiles from the sky.

Lizyin (GM): Chandler manages to shoot all of them but one, the final one slipping through the Sunflower's defense screen and rocking the ship. The console behind Dr. Conley explodes.

Dr. Donovan Conley: ((Does that mean I'm supposed to take damage? How does this work?))

Lizyin (GM):((Write up what seems appropriate.))

Dr. Donovan Conley: The console exploded, sending Donovan flying across the bridge. He slammed into a bulkhead, falling to the ground.

Veela: "Doctor! Someone help him!"

Lt. Chandler: Chandler, seeing no further missiles incoming, moved from his station to crouch at the doctor's side. "Big hit you took. You okay?"

Lizyin (GM): The doctor would have a minor concussion and some burn wounds on the back of his legs.

Dr. Donovan Conley: He felt pretty woozy, but he wasn't out yet. He touched his head as it pounded. "Can you get me my medical bag?"

Lt. Chandler: He hurried over to the bag by the exploded console, picking it up and bringing it over to the doctor.

Dr. Donovan Conley: Once the bag was there, he grabbed his regenerator and ran it across his leg where the burns were.

Lizyin (GM): The burns heal slowly.

Veela: She stood from her seat and made her way to the doctor. "Are you going to be okay?"

Dr. Donovan Conley: "My head is swimming, but I'll survive."

Veela: She put a reassuring hand on his shoulder before heading back to her captain's chair. "Alright. Looks like we dealt with their defenses. What do we see?"

Ray Athan: He took a reading with the ship's sensors.

Lizyin (GM): You see a lush, green planet. There are ruins on the northern continent. There are signs of several beasts both on the ground and in the air on the planet, but no sign of current civilization.

Ray Athan: "Looks like an overgrown planet. Might be some potential danger with the creatures down there, but nothing aside from ruins otherwise."

Veela: "Unless there's traps."

Lt. Chandler: He returned to his station. "There's almost certainly traps."

Veela: She called engineering on her comms. "How are the systems looking?"

Aria Benoit: [Comms] "Only minor damage. Everything seems to be a go."

Veela: "Okay. Prepare the ship for landing. And doc, I hope you're gonna be up to it soon cuz we're gonna need all the bodies we can down there on the planet."

Dr. Donovan Conley: "I'll do what I can." He found pain medication in his bag and took it for the head injury.

Lizyin (GM): ((Alright, we'll continue this next week, sound good?))

Veela: ((Aye.))

#DM-Dr.-Donovan-Conley

Dr. Donovan Conley: This is so cool. Thank you for being so welcoming.

Veela: Sorry you got hurt on your first outing!

Dr. Donovan Conley: No worries. Was neat being involved in the action. Otherwise I'd have been just sitting there.

Veela: lol true.

Dr. Donovan Conley: Do you know when the next scene is?

Veela: They try to plan them when we're all online. Just check #General

Dr. Donovan Conley: Sounds good.

Veela: Have a good night.

Dr. Donovan Conley: you too.

4

Jason

Jason lay awake in bed for the rest of the evening, staring at his ceiling. Despite having light, comfortable sheets for the summer, and one of those fancy online-bought pillows which were supposed to keep cooler than the standard stuff, he found he couldn't stop his mind from working.

The game was too fun. Maybe he'd only been able to treat his wounds as a doctor, but it was still exciting. It was amazing how so many people could operate and work on a plot together to make it unfold like that. He'd always thought about trying his hand at writing but never really had the discipline to write an entire novel. This collaborative process was a lot more fun.

And he found himself liking Veela.

She had a take-charge attitude, something different than he'd seen in most women—assuming she was a woman in real life. He thought about how to ask her the question tactfully. Perhaps he could ask her name and find out that way.

His thoughts had drifted more to her, and he found himself chuckling. Why did he care what some random name online thought of him? He liked how she smiled over at him in the game, and she seemed willing to talk afterward.

He shifted in his bed, letting his arm slide behind his pillow. It would eventually fall asleep in that position, but it felt comfortable for the time being. He hated these times of the evening, being alone, when having someone next to him would have been nice. He used to have Danielle, but she'd hated when he'd moved up to Reno. She couldn't adjust to the slower-paced lifestyle compared to LA.

But still, he found he missed her. At least, he missed having company. He couldn't help but be lonely.

Part of him wanted to log back on and see if Veela were still awake, but she probably wasn't. It was too late for him as it was. He had to be up with the markets in the morning, and there was no way he'd get a full night's sleep.

The game occupied him and gave him a little companionship, but he still was lonely. It seemed he couldn't win.

Eventually, Jason resolved to stop thinking and do his best to go to sleep. He forced his eyes shut and tried to clear his mind, but all he could think of was when he could play with Veela next.

He wondered what she was thinking.

Rachel

Finally, the game was taking off. There were over a hundred players in different regions of the game, and many of them had their own storylines, but Rachel had been trying to get the Sunflower flying for months and couldn't scrape up enough layers to run a mission.

What luck the last few days had been. It gave her a much-needed distraction from work and her parents. If only she could be a real starship captain and float amongst the stars, trying to find a strange orb as a remnant of old alien civilizations.

But it was just fantasy. She had to remember that and not get too hooked on the game. At her internship, she'd gone a little overboard and lost a full-time position for a multinational corporation as their cross-cultural liaison. She'd shown up late one too many times, which killed her ambitions of doing the work she wanted, forcing her into a position where she had to waitress just to stay afloat.

She wouldn't ask her parents for money or move back in with them like they wanted. Rachel had too much pride for that and tried to make it on her own. Being beholden to anyone, even to her parents, sounded terrible.

All good things would end at some point, but for now, she could at least take small solace in the fun she had while she took more time to figure things out.

The job listings webpage loomed in front of her. She had submitted her resume to a couple of places—jobs in San Francisco, D.C., but so far, she'd not made it out of the first round of applicants. It felt like she spun her wheels, trying repeatedly without results, but something had to hit eventually. Once the economy settled back in.

She'd been telling herself that for the last year, but nothing had been moving for her. Rachel could feel the twist of depression creeping back into her gut. Something she couldn't allow to take hold. If she spiraled into one of those cycles now, she would hardly make it to work, and she couldn't afford to lose this job and still keep the apartment.

Idly, Rachel clicked over to the Space Adventure Online page, scrolling through the recent chat. It was late, so only a few Euro players were still on, leaving the game dead. But she fell upon her D.M.s with Conley—or Jas868 as he had originally been on the chat. He was certainly friendly, or at least liked to be chatty. It was fun. It had been a while since she'd made a close friend on the game. Lizyin, the G.M., had probably been her closest. That's why she was able to get such an interesting plot. It paid to be friends with the boss, even though Lizyin did all she could to be impartial, Rachel knew.

This friendship would be different, though, as there would be no G.M./Player dynamic. She could talk to this Jas guy like he was a regular person. It was nice.

Finally, she closed her laptop. The game could wait for

another day, and so could the job listings. There was nothing to get impatient about while she could still pay her rent, despite her family putting pressure on her.

\#Aethon

Lizyin (GM):The party stepped off of the ship into a lush tropical forest. There were remnants of statues with broken off faces around. Vines tangled around them. The area had been overgrown for some time.

Veela: Veela led first. Perhaps it wasn't the best idea for a captain to do so, but she liked to show her crew she wasn't afraid to work. She scanned the area. "Okay, people. Stay sharp. If you see anything that looks like an Orb of Reckoning, let me know." '

Lt. Chandler: "Oh, I'm sure we're going to have to descend into some pit to get that. It's how these things tend to go." He kept his eyes peeled for threats.

Ray Athan: The rogue grinned as he joined his companions. "Might be some other loot worth grabbing too."

Dr. Donovan Conley: The doctor moved with the rest

of the party, his bag of instruments and medicines slung around his side in case of an emergency. This was a much more frightening prospect than simply standing around in an operating room.

Aria Benoit: The engineer joined the crew, finally, holding up a scanning instrument to attempt to find a path toward any interesting objects.

Lizyin (GM): Aria would find what appeared to be an ancient road beneath their feet. Stone was in the ground, but overgrown with vegetation and dirt covering the majority of it. It led forward into a deeper forest.

Aria Benoit: "Captain I think I found a literal path forward. Follow me." She trekked into the vegetation.

Veela: Veela followed Aria.

Lt. Chandler: He drew his pulse pistol, sensing there would probably be danger going forward.

Ray Athan: Ray followed Chandler's lead while flanking the group on the other side.

Dr. Donovan Conley: Don followed along, hoping they wouldn't be headed toward their doom.

Lizyin (GM): Eventually, they came upon the ruins of a temple, which looked a lot like the Mayan pyramids on Earth, severely weathered, vegetation everywhere. Giant spiders crawled along its stones, nearly a third of the size of a human being.

Dr. Donovan Conley: "These spiders give me the creeps."

Veela: She observed them. "They don't appear to be attacking us. Probably scarier than they look. Is there a way inside?"

Aria Benoit: She held her device up to the pyramid.

Lizyin (GM): Aria spots a doorway around to the left side which will give them access.

Aria Benoit: "Follow me again." She led off the path, crunching on leaves as she walked toward the opening.

Veela: Veela followed until they arrived, then she put on her flashlight and looked inside.

Lizyin (GM): The captain would see stone carvings in the rocks on the inside, representations that looked a lot like human sacrifice.

Lt. Chandler: He arrived in time to spot the drawings. "Creepy."

Ray Athan: "Well, here goes nothing." He arrived at the entrance.

Dr. Donovan Conley: He wasn't too sure about this, the doctor very much out of his element.

Veela: Veela patted the doctor on the arm. "Look alive, doctor, because I bet it's going to get crazier from here."

Lizyin (GM): ((Alright, everyone. I need to head in for work. We'll pick this up later.))

Veela: ((See you!))

#DM-Veela

Dr. Donovan Conley: I feel like it always stops just as it's about to get interesting.

Veela: I know it. How are you?

Dr. Donovan Conley: Great, you?

Veela: A little tired. Sick of work.

Dr. Donovan Conley: Aren't we all. Take a vacation?

Veela: I wish I had the money to be able to afford it.

Dr. Donovan Conley: Ahh, sorry.

Veela: Not your fault.

Dr. Donovan Conley: Where are you from, anyway?

Veela: Nashville. You?

Dr. Donovan Conley: Reno. Way less fun than your town.

Veela: You'd think. Everywhere gets old and everyone always thinks the grass is greener elsewhere.

Dr. Donovan Conley: I don't mind where I live. Nashville though is a real party city.

Veela: If you're not working. The downtown bars district is a lot less fun for locals. There are only so many bachelorette parties we can handle.

Dr. Donovan Conley: Ha. True. Well, I still find it cool.

Veela: Suit yourself. I'd love to be somewhere like Paris or London personally.

Dr. Donovan Conley: Those are fancy places. What makes you think there?

Veela: My degree. I want to travel internationally as much as possible and see the world. There's so much to explore.

Dr. Donovan Conley: Travel and living are two different things.

Veela: Yeah, but you get a real feel for a city after a few months there, when you're not a tourist.

Dr. Donovan Conley: I suppose you're right.

Veela: Anyway, gotta get going. Later!

Dr. Donovan Conley: Bye!

5

Jason

Jason parked his white Porsche GT4 at the parking stall closest to the front of the Somersett Country Club. He had an uncanny ability to get good parking places, and today proved no exception as he would meet one of his local competitors, Ryan Alden, for their monthly lunch meeting.

A competitor wasn't the correct term, as Jason wasn't striving to get any new clients, nor was Ryan attempting to take any from him. They both managed financial investments, however, and they could talk shop and figure out what new mutual funds to target and where to avoid together. Better to band together with information than to go it alone. Jason kept in touch with several people in the industry similarly.

The country club still had a dress code of a collared shirt and no jeans for men, so Jason had to wear a baby blue polo with his khaki slacks. He hated dressing up like this but understood how the club wanted to maintain a standard of decor.

He walked up a spiral staircase to large glass doors, pulling them open to step inside. The club was decorated in a lavish yet classic style reminiscent of the early 1900s. It had art on the golf course wall and celebrity champions who had come through there over the years before opening to a hallway where they had their bar and the restaurant beyond that.

Jason greeted the hostess, who informed him Ryan was already ahead of him, and he made his way to his table.

Ryan stood, shaking Jason's hand with an overly-enthusiastic firm grip. "Hey, man. Long time."

"Yeah, sorry I missed our last lunch." Jason shifted his gaze over the golf course, where their seat provided a prime view of the first tee. As he took his seat, a group was warming up to start their game.

"All good; I know how these things go. Getting harder to get out with the kids," Ryan said, resuming his chair.

"You've got two now?" Jason asked, feeling slightly guilty for not remembering Ryan's personal life enough, but Jason had always been lost in his own world.

"Three. Maggie's the youngest. Just started sleeping through the night," Ryan said.

"Well, thank God for small miracles," Jason said, taking the menu into his hand and looking it over. He wasn't hungry but decided he'd grab the light spring salad and add some chicken.

"How about you? You meet anyone new yet?" Ryan had been around doing the ugly divorce, memories Jason didn't particularly want to relive.

Jason shifted uncomfortably in his chair, though for the first time since he could remember when he'd been asked the question, he didn't think of Danielle. Instead, his mind went to Veela. How did she get into his head? "Not exactly."

Ryan smirked at him. "Not exactly means you're thinking about it. My man. About time, if you ask me.

Shouldn't let the wicked witch keep you holed up in your house alone forever."

The topic made him more than uncomfortable, though Jason played it off with a small smile to try to be friendly.

"What are you seeing action-wise for the S&P?" Jason changed the topic to business, hoping Ryan wouldn't notice.

Ryan was ready for it, taking out an iPad and showing Jason the latest statistics on several companies, both up and down. Jason's clients didn't like to short companies, but it was good to know the trajectories of different industries nonetheless.

They ordered and continued their conversation, Jason then reciprocating the information by handing Ryan a few printouts of his own. "Commodities are going insane, as much as I hate putting down money there. I've shifted the portfolios by about five percent recently, though. It's a good hedge."

"I've done the same," Ryan said.

Their food arrived, and they ate, continuing the business talk. Several rounds of golfers passed by. Sometimes, Ryan would pressure Jason into having a cocktail or two with lunch, but today both seemed to be on the same page about wanting to get back to work after they were done.

"Oh, yeah. I forgot to tell you. There's going to be an independent brokers convention in about three weeks. It'd be awesome to introduce you to some of my friends from back east," Ryan said.

"I don't do conventions. They're just excuses to get boozed up," Jason said. "Rarely do anything for business."

Ryan laughed. "You know it's all about connections. Live a little."

"Maybe," Jason said hesitantly. "Where is it at?"

"Music City. Nashville, Tennessee."

What a coincidence. Hadn't Veela just mentioned she was from there the night prior? His mind raced with the idea of actually getting to see her. But would she even want to? They'd just started talking. It might be too weird.

"You're thinking about it." Ryan grinned.

"I am."

"Well, let me know. I'll make sure they hold you a spot. But, hey, I've got a meeting at one thirty across town. Would you mind covering, and I'll get you next time?" Ryan asked, pushing back his chair and placing his napkin on the table.

"Oh. Sure." Jason didn't mind. He tended to pick up the bill anyway, which he liked doing for his friends. Money wasn't much of an object for him, and he liked to give when he could.

"Great. See you in Nashville." Ryan stood and gave him a big grin before turning to head out.

"I didn't say I was going yet!" Jason called after him.

"You didn't have to. I saw it in your eyes!"

Space Adventures Online

#Aethon

—

Lizyin (GM): ((Okay, I'm here. Everyone ready?))

Veela: ((Yes!))

Veela: Veela stepped inside the large opening, flashlight ahead of her, hand on her pistol and ready to grab her pulse pistol.

Lt. Chandler: Chandler was close behind her. "I wish you'd let me take point, captain."

Veela: "Nonsense. This is my mission. I'm going to lead."

Dr. Donovan Conley: He stuck to Veela's side opposite Chandler.

Ray Athan: Ray was happy to be further back. If they encountered something dangerous, he'd get a much better look.

Aria Benoit: Aria followed.

Lizyin (GM): They wound into a tight corridor which went down, down, down. Spider webs hung everywhere.

Lt. Chandler: "Why do I get the feeling we're heading into the nest of one of those nasty things that are going to be ten times the size of the ones we saw outside?"

Veela: "Probably because we are. But we have pulse weapons and those spiders won't." Veela continued forward.

Lizyin (GM): Veela passes a small slit in the wall where an axe swoops across.

Dr. Donovan Conley: "Veela!" He jumped forward, tackling her to get her out of the way of the axe.

Lt. Chandler: "Hey, that's my job." Chandler held his pulse pistol, wryly speaking as it seemed Conley had taken care of matters.

Veela: Veela fell to the ground in front of the axe, hitting with a thud, scraping her hands on the floor when she braced herself. She turned and scrambled with Conley on top of her, gazing at him for a long moment.

Dr. Donovan Conley: He was so close to her he could smell the scent of her hair. It made him freeze, realizing how beautiful the captain was.

Ray Athan: ((Get a room, you two! Lol))

Veela: She stayed there a little longer before pushing at his chest with her hand. "You're heavy."

Dr. Donovan Conley: "Oh, right, sorry." He chuckled before rolling off of her and getting to his feet. When he did, he offered her a hand up.

Veela: Veela took it, getting back to her feet before dusting herself off. She looked around. "Everyone alright?"

Aria Benoit: "Looks like you took the worst of it."

Veela: "Okay, then let's keep going."

Lt. Chandler: "I really think you should let me take point. It's my job." Chandler spoke firmly.

Veela: She nodded. "Okay. I guess you're right. Then you can deal with the poison darts and big rock tumbling down about to smash us all."

Dr. Donovan Conley: Conley laughed.

#DM-Dr-Donovan-Conley:

Dr. Donovan Conley: You're hilarious. I love that movie and this totally feels like we're in an old adventure.

Veela: Thought it was appropriate.

Dr. Donovan Conley: This game is so much fun I can hardly bclicvc it cxists.

Veela: You get used to it after awhile. But yeah, it's very different. It's a good stress relief. I find it relaxing.

Dr. Donovan Conley: Agreed. Hey, you said you were out in Nashville, right?

Veela: Yeah.

Dr. Donovan Conley: I'm sorry if this is weird, but it turns out I'll be headed to a Nashville for work in a few days. Do you want to get together?

Rachel

Do you want to get together?

Rachel froze at her laptop. For a moment, she forgot to breathe. She had never thought of someone on the chat coming to her neighborhood or being nearby. The idea was too much for her. She found herself biting her nails in her nervousness.

How should she reply? She didn't know who was on the other side of the screen at all. He could be a monstrosity or some serial killer trying to murder her. Why had she ever told someone she lived in Nashville?

Despite herself, she found herself typing a response. I don't know anything about you. How old are you?

Why did she ask that? It would only encourage him, and she wasn't ready for this.

Rachel closed her laptop in a hurry, not wanting to see his reply just yet. She was supposed to go to lunch with Jenny from work, have a little girl talk, gossip about life, and get her mind off things. But now all she could think of was this guy asking to see her.

She laughed to herself. He knew nothing about her too.

For all he knew, she was another guy like him playing a character. Asking her out wasn't targeted or something to worry about.

Her phone buzzed, Jenny, letting her know she would be fifteen minutes late. The girl was always late, even to work, so Rachel had been budgeting it into her time anyway. Even Chris, her manager, started scheduling her shift fifteen minutes early to make up for it. Jenny was well-liked by the customers, getting a lot of tips, so he tolerated her bad habits.

Rachael hurried into the bathroom, brushed her hair, threw a scrunchie on to ensure it stayed put, and ran out the door. A moment later, she realized she'd forgotten her car keys and ran back inside to grab them off the small side table by the front door and headed out of her apartment again. She locked the door behind her and took off.

But once she got to her car, she couldn't help but start thinking about this whole offer Conley had made her—or rather, Conley's player had made. It was hard to think of him as anything different than his screen name; it was all she knew about him.

She swiped up on her phone to pull up the chat room. Space Adventures Online was harder to use on a phone than a laptop, so she preferred to log on at home, but she couldn't help but be curious if Conley replied.

She had a DM from him and opened it up.

Space Adventures Online

#DM-Dr-Donovan-Conley:

———

Veela: I know nothing about you. I don't even know your real name.

Dr. Donovan Conley: Oh! Jeez, I don't even think about that. Sorry. I'm new. My name's Jason. I'm 30. I'm an investment manager and there's a convention out there in a couple of weeks, just thought it might be cool to get a coffee or something.

Veela: I'm Rachel, 23. Let me think about it. I've never met anyone from online before.

Dr. Donovan Conley: Me either.

Veela: Hey, look. I gotta go. We'll talk later. K?

Dr. Donovan Conley: Sounds good to me.

———

#General

Ray Athan: I am so bored but I'm stuck in a scene.

Lizyin (GM): You could make an alt and play casual back on the station?

Ray Athan: Ehh, I'm good. Only vibing this.

Dr. Donovan Conley: What's an alt?

Lizyin (GM): It's an alternative character. A lot of people play multiple in case they get stuck in RP waiting and want to do something else.

Dr. Donovan Conley: Oh, cool.

Lizyin (GM): As a GM it's easy because I get to play all the NPCs. :)

Ray Athan: Jealous. I hope Veela's ship is active enough to where I'm not bored all the time.

Dr. Donovan Conley: Me too. Though I don't know much different.

Ray Athan: A few months ago we had a ship of 20 people on the server. Was pretty cool.

Dr. Donovan Conley: Sounds like a lot to remember.

Ray Athan: You get used to it. Veela was ops officer on that before starting her own deal. It kinda died later.

Dr. Donovan Conley: Cool.

#DM-Ray-Athan

Dr. Donovan Conley: Hey.

Ray Athan: What's poppin'?

Dr. Donovan Conley: Are you good friends with Veela?

Ray Athan: I guess? I've played with her for about a year.

Dr. Donovan Conley: Is she pretty cool?

Ray Athan: … Not sure what you mean. She's nice enough and doesn't really cause drama. You should see some of the players on here when they don't get what they want. Kinda weird questions, though I gotta say.

Dr. Donovan Conley: Sorry, just trying to figure something out.

Ray Athan: Ahh. You like her. Haha

Dr. Donovan Conley: I barely know her, just curious is all.

Ray Athan: Suuuuuuure. She mostly keeps to herself OOC. Don't know a lot.

Dr. Donovan Conley: OOC?

Ray Athan: You really are a noob. Out Of Character.

Dr. Donovan Conley: Oh, right. That makes sense. Yeah. Well thanks, I guess.

Ray Athan: No prob.

6

Jason

Jason tried to get back to work, but he could hardly focus. The screen looked like a blur, the emails too long to read. His phone lit up with calls from his clients, but he could only think about Veela.

Had he overstepped by asking to see her? The game was so fun, their adventure such a new experience he didn't want to jeopardize it. This all started with a brief flirtatious moment in-game, where he'd had his character dive atop hers. He'd felt such an exciting sensation then, reminding him of going to school, talking to a high school crush at a locker between classes.

He could picture it back then, recalling Melinda, her sparkling eyes shining at him with the happiest and most innocent smiles. In many ways, he pictured Veela in the same manner, even though she was, in reality, a character in the text on a screen.

Did other people get sensations from their characters like this? How crazy must he be to get a crush on someone who wasn't real, based on an avatar, which wasn't real? It made him laugh in a self-deprecating manner. He'd been alone too long, focused on his work, avoiding real contact with people.

Yes, he had his clients, trainer, and even work friends like Ryan, who he saw regularly, but there was no deep connection. He didn't fit in, and if it weren't for his business or his money, would any of them be around? Likely not.

The game interactions were purer in that regard. No one knew who he was or what he had. Veela didn't think he had anything to offer her other than his intellect in developing a fantastic story to build with their characters. She had no expectations of him. It was freeing to him.

He'd not tried to build any relationship since Danielle. It was supposed to have been forever. They had the American dream—a big house, money enough to do what they wanted, and travel where they wanted, and yet for some reason, it had felt so empty. It never satisfied them.

They'd grown distant in the last couple of years, and finally, they had to have the talk where it wasn't working anymore. She'd moved out and left him here.

He tried hard not to think about it, to keep himself occupied. For a while, he'd gone out on dates and had shallow relationships with beautiful women, but they could never authentically connect with him. All he wanted was a real connection.

Why did it have to be so complicated?

He hoped he hadn't blown it with Veela by moving too fast. He'd just asked to go to coffee, but it felt like such a more enormous step than it should have been. He'd have done the same if he'd met her at the supermarket or the club. Why did this feel so different?

It was partly because he could already tell Veela was more intelligent than most other women he'd talked to.

Moreover, she was a gem of genuine creativity, something rare in the modern world.

The truth hit him like a ten-ton truck. He was pining over this girl on the internet and wanted her. This was a recipe for disaster.

Space Adventures Online

#Aethon

◻

Lizyin (GM): The party descended into the depths of the pyramid, which had a robust underground network of catacombs. It was dark, the air stale like no one had been here in perhaps thousands of years.

Dr. Donovan Conley: ((Should we wait for Veela?))

Lizyin (GM): ((This is all the time I have today. She's out with a friend and said it's fine.))

Ray Athan: ((Happens. Sometimes you just gotta play.))

Dr. Donovan Conley: Don continued down the corridors with his flashlight on, getting an eerie feeling from this place. "How do we even find this orb thing?"

Ray Athan: "I'm going to guess it's going to be at the very bottom in some kind of crypt. I wonder what's up in the pyramid, though." He followed along.

Lt. Chandler: "More spiders, probably." He kept his eyes peeled for threats as usual.

Lizyin (GM): They came upon a thick cobweb blocking their path.

Lt. Chandler: ((I shouldn't have said anything.))

Dr. Donovan Conley: "I'm not going first. I'm just a doctor."

Lt. Chandler: "I think you should do the honors, Ray. You're our six-hundred credit pilot and guide, after all." He gave a bright smile.

Ray Athan: The rogue grumbled, but pulled out of his pack a small lighter. "I knew this would come in handy." He flicked it to create a flame and then held it to the web.

Lizyin (GM): The web lit on fire, slowly melting away, but behind it a giant spider was very mad that her nest was destroyed! She skittered toward the group, clearly attacking.

Dr. Donovan Conley: Don stumbled backward behind everyone.

Lt. Chandler: Chandler calmly drew his pulse pistol and fired several shots into the spider.

Ray Athan: Ray waved his lighter at the spider, trying to get it to catch flame just like the web had.

Lizyin (GM): The pulse pistol shots staggered the spider, making it crumple to the ground on its legs and shriek with a piercing sound. Ray's lighter then hit it and it caught aflame, smelling of rotten flesh as it twitched and stopped moving.

Lt. Chandler: Chandler walked up to the spider just to make sure there were no tricks and then nodded. "This is why you bring a trained security officer. No problem."

Dr. Donovan Conley: "Let's get this over with before more of its friends come by." He scooted around the spider-a-flambe, and kept going.

Ray Athan: Rya followed Conley. "Surprised you're taking the lead, doctor."

Dr. Donovan Conley: "Someone has to." He shrugged.

Lt. Chandler: Chandler escorted his team down the corridor, eyes peeled for more traps or problems.

Lizyin (GM): Eventually, the party came to an end of the corridor, a big door which was sealed.

Aria Benoit: ((Sorry guys, just got home. Can I still join?))

Ray Athan: ((Aria got bit by a giant spider and died. Sorry.))

Aria Benoit: ((Har, har.))

Dr. Donovan Conley: ((We can just say you were with us the whole time.))

Aria Benoit: ((Thanks.))

Aria Benoit: Aria stepped up to the door, scanning it with her device to see if there were any obvious way to open it.

Lizyin (GM): The ancient ruins were strange and the door was electrified with some current.

Dr. Donovan Conley: "What do you see?" Donovan asked, not going to touch the door yet.

Aria Benoit: "Seems like another trap, like an electric fence but not. I'm going to set my scanner to overload and put it against it and see if I can't short it."

Lt. Chandler: "But then we won't be able to use your device anymore."

Aria Benoit: She shrugged. "All part of the job." She then tapped her controls on her scanning device, setting the overload before bending down to slide the gadget against the bottom of the door.

Lizyin (GM): It went off, and it shorted out the door. The rock face of the door crumpled when the current died opening into what appeared to be an ancient crypt with a sealed sarcophagus.

Lizyin (GM): ((I think we should stop here for now and wait for Veela))
Dr. Donovan Conley: ((Yeah.))
Lt. Chandler: ((Good by me.))

#DM-Veela

Dr. Donovan Conley: Hey, we made it to the chamber. Wish you got to play with us and hope you're having fun out with your friend. See you soon!

Rachel

Rachel's phone buzzed on the table. She'd set it up to get notifications when she received DMs from the chat and forgotten to turn it off when she'd left.

Jenny glanced at the phone. "I've seen you eyeballing it all lunch. Is there something going on? Did you meet someone?"

Rachel dabbed her napkin against her lips and set it down. She didn't want to check it. If she explained she'd been sitting around playing some online science fiction roleplaying chat game, it would be about the most embarrassing thing she could think of. She loved the chat, but the idea of it was so nerdy. Jenny would laugh at her, and Rachel didn't want to feel self-conscious.

"No," Rachel said. "Just a friend, I'm sure."

The response made Jenny's eyes twinkle. "Just a friend. You sound defensive."

There was no getting past her. Jenny was to gossip like white on rice. The girl had a knack for digging into every little detail about a person's life. It made for great conversations as Rachel spent the lunch learning about her boss and coworkers and their intimate secrets, which they thought no one knew. It would be a matter of time before Jenny learned about Space Adventures Online and spread the word to the whole bar.

The embarrassment crept onto Rachel's face as she flushed despite herself.

"I knew it," Jenny said, setting down her fork. "Spill the beans."

Rachel twirled the end of her hair, self-conscious and under a spotlight. It tugged, and she knew it would end up in a knot, but she couldn't help her jittery reflexes.

"Alright. I started talking to this guy online," Rachel said.

"Studly Mingle Dot Com?" Jenny teased.

"No, I'm not on a dating site. It's like a shared hobby with this book series I like."

"That sounds more like you."

Rachel couldn't be sure if Jenny meant to compliment or criticize her, so she shook her head and continued. "Anyway, he's not from around here, but he's coming out for some work convention in a couple of weeks. He wants to meet up for coffee."

"Then we need to go down to Midtown and get you a nice sundress."

Rachel waved Jenny off. "No. I haven't decided if I'm going to do it or not yet. It's weird."

"Why? Just meet in a public place, park somewhere well-lit, and make sure he doesn't follow you. If you don't want him to follow you, that is. Otherwise, you can have him go back to your place." Jenny smirked.

"I'm not that kind of girl," Rachel protested.

"I know. I'm teasing. But you should do it. You haven't gone on a date since I've known you, and it'll do good for you."

"I don't know." The idea scared her. Too many potential date outcomes crept into her head which ended in disaster. But the worst part was, what if she decided she liked him? He didn't live anywhere near here. She didn't want a long-distance relationship. It would be painful not to be near someone and dating.

"Look, the worst that can happen is you don't like the guy that much, and you send him on his way with a thank you very much. Have a great life." Jenny remained all smiles.

"You don't think it's unsafe?"

"Look, if it makes you happier, I can sit in the coffee shop, look after you, and call the cops if anything shady goes down. But it probably won't. People meet online all the time. It sounds fun."

Rachel sucked in her bottom lip, more nervous now than when Jenny forced her into the conversation. "I'll think about it."

Space Adventures Online

#General

Veela: Sorry I missed the event today, all.

Lizyin (GM): Veela! <3 No problem. Real life comes first.

Ray Athan: It was fun. Would have been more fun if Aria would have actually gotten bitten by a giant spider.

Aria Benoit: You're lucky Aria doesn't take one as a pet and drop it in your quarters when it's hungry.

Lt. Chandler: Our new doctor kinda took charge. You might be in the running to get replaced as captain.

Veela: Oh?

Dr. Donovan Conley: I could never replace her. :)

Ray Athan: Simp.

Dr. Donovan Conley: What's that supposed mean?

Lizyin (GM): Alright guys, don't get heated. I'm sure it's just being playful.

Ray Athan: You know it. Why's everyone gotta get all

serious all the time?

Dr. Donovan Conley: It's okay. I'm not offended.

Veela: Oh, nice, looks like we just got to the end.

Lizyin (GM): You'll have to wait and see.

Veela: @Aria Benoit. Do you have some more time tonight? Maybe we can finish up.

Aria Benoit: Here!

Lizyin (GM): Well, I have time. Everyone ready?

Dr. Donovan Conley: Let's go.

#Aethon

Veela: Veela had been hanging back and letting her team do their jobs, but she came to the chambers and entered the room first, unafraid. "I bet the orb is in the sarcophagus."

Aria Benoit: "I wish I had my scanner to analyze it." She lamented having to overload it to open the door.

Lt. Chandler: "We'll have to open it the old fashioned way." He clutched his pulse weapon tightly like it was a prized possession.

Veela: Veela bit her lip, trying to think of the safest way to manage things. "Aria, why don't you and Ray pull the lid off. Chandler, have your pulse pistol at the ready in case there's something in there that needs shooting."

Ray Athan: He walked to the sarcophagus. "I have to be the tank now?"

Aria Benoit: "I'm the tank, dummy. Cybernetic arm. You just keep this balanced. Ready?" She grabbed one corner of the sarcophagus.

Ray Athan: He grabbed the other.

Dr. Donovan Conley: Conley hung back and watched. He'd fix their wounds later if need be.

Veela: Veela glanced at the doctor. "Sorry there's not a lot for you to do. But that's a good thing."

Dr. Donovan Conley: "It is. I'd rather be ready than tending to serious wounds."

Veela: She nodded. "Alright, on my mark."

Lt. Chandler: He pointed his pulse pistol at the sarcophagus.

Veela: "Mark!"

Ray Athan: He lifted.

Aria Benoit: She lifted.

Lizyin (GM): The sarcophagus opened, dust kicking into the air. It had been sealed for thousands of years. Bones lay inside, but so did a round, obsidian object. No monsters popped out. It appeared they were safe— for now.

Veela: Veela stepped forward and grabbed the orb. "This is it."

Lt. Chandler: "You should have let me handle it in case there's something amiss with it."

Ray Athan: He set the lid down. "This was easy."

Aria Benoit: "Too easy." She followed his lead.

Dr. Donovan Conley: He scanned the area, not noticing anything amiss. "We should get back to the ship."

Veela: ((Anything else, GM?))

Lizyin (GM): ((Nope, you guys are good to go!))

Veela: She nodded. "Alright. Let's get out of here. Good work, everyone. Time to get back to Palmer Station and get paid." She carried the orb outside of the room and made her way back through this maze toward their ship. Hopefully they remembered where they parked.

7

Jason

"Let's hit those skull crushers," Tim said, clapping several times while standing over the bench where Jason laid down.

He had two thirty-five pound dumbbells in his hands, arms straight up, but forearms bent back over his head. This weight was challenging. He could feel the strain near his elbows, only exacerbated by the typing he'd been doing lately. He couldn't return the conversation while he straightened his arms up and let them drop again. His triceps flexed and burned, but they were getting bigger, and the weight he could lift was increasing over the last couple of months. Progress.

"You're really getting at it today," Tim said as Jason finished his set.

Once done, Jason let the weights fall onto his chest. Tim grabbed one and set it off to the side, which allowed Jason to move the other and sit up again.

"Yeah. I'm energized."

"Girl?"

"Huh?"

Jason thought about it. He'd heard Tim but wasn't prepared for the question. Sweat dripped down his brow from the exertion, but he wiped it away with his sleeve.

"Yeah, actually," Jason said.

"Always good motivation. She pretty?" Tim asked, grabbing a lighter weight so Jason could follow up with some flies.

He always felt like a wimp when he took the twenty-pound dumbbells for flies. They seemed so easy on the first reps, but by the time he got to thirty, his chest would be burning, especially after pushing through all of the tricep work right before. However, the exercise still wasn't as difficult, and he could talk through it.

"I don't know," Jason said.

Tim laughed. "What do you mean you don't know? Does that mean she's a butterface?"

"No, I legitimately don't know. I'm talking to her online."

"Well, what's her pic look like?" Tim asked.

Jason reached those final reps, having to finish and breathe before he could reply.

"I don't know. Never seen one. It's all been through like a chatroom," Jason said. It felt weird to talk about. How could he be interested in someone he didn't even know what she looked like? She seemed smart and together, and that enticed him. He wanted to talk to her more, but she hadn't replied to his DMs since he'd sent the last one, and he didn't want to come across as overbearing.

All he could do was wait. Wait and check his DMs over and over. It made him feel like a chump, but what could he do?

"That's... pretty out there," Tim said, taking these weights away from him. "I think we crushed your tris and chest enough for the day. You feeling good?"

"Yeah. I'm gonna be sore," Jason said.

"Then I did my job."

Jason let out a deep breath, tired from the workout. He had left his phone downstairs, which he regretted since he wanted to check if Veela had messaged him. Maybe he was a simp, as Ray had told him. It made him chuckle to himself.

Tim gave him a pat on the shoulder. "Well, find out what this girl looks like before getting too deep. I mean text; she might not even be a girl."

"Oh, come on."

"Never know." Tim smirked.

Jason threw his towel at his trainer. "Jerk."

Space Adventures Online

Dr. Donovan Conley: Hey all.

Ray Athan: 'Sup.

Lt. Chandler: Hey doctor.

Dr. Donovan Conley: What's going on?

Lt. Chandler: Not much. Lizyin's out today so I guess there won't really be a game.

Dr. Donovan Conley: That's too bad. I just got done with my workout. I've got a lot of energy and my mind's ready to be creative.

Ray Athan: Beefing up for @Veela?

Dr. Donovan Conley: Funny. I try to keep myself in shape for my own health benefits.

Veela: Leave him alone, Ray.

Ray Athan: I swear all of you are way too sensitive. Plus he's a simp.

Dr. Donovan Conley: Well, she's the captain. Isn't it good to make the boss happy?

Ray Athan: Knew it.

Dr. Donovan Conley: Whatever. Well, we don't really need a GM to play on the ship, right? We can just play?

Ray Athan: Meh.

Lt. Chandler: I gotta get going in a few anyway. I'll be on for the next scene.

Veela: I can play with you if you'd like.

Dr. Donovan Conley: Cool.

#Sunflower

Veela: Veela sat in her ready room office, just beside the bridge. It had been a long walk down to the ruins and back again, and she was tired from the adventure. She held the orb in her hand over her desk, pondering why this could be so valuable.

Dr. Donovan Conley: He rang the chime to her door, standing in front of it. His heart raced with some nervousness, though he wasn't sure why.

Veela: She looked up. "Come in."

Dr. Donovan Conley: Don walked through the door, noting the orb in her hand. "I had expected something a little more showy for an ancient object everyone's after."

Veela: "Me too. It's like we're missing a piece of the puzzle, but I can't figure it out." She set the orb down on her desk, giving him a warm smile. "Come in. Do you want some tea or anything?"

Dr. Donovan Conley: "I'm good." He moved over and

took a seat as she'd told him. He tried to be relaxed yet respectful.

Veela: "How are you enjoying the assignment?"

Dr. Donovan Conley: "Not too bad. Not a lot of action other than tending to myself. I feel like I haven't really earned my pay." He chuckled.

Veela: "It wasn't your fault a console blew up beside you."

Dr. Donovan Conley: "No, I guess not. But still, I'm here to heal, right?"

Veela: "You're here as insurance in case we need healing. It's better if we don't. I don't mind the expense." She smiled at him warmly.

Dr. Donovan Conley: "Well, good. I don't want to be a burden to you." He looked her in the eyes.

Veela: The way he looked at her gave her some pause. "I don't think you would be."

Dr. Donovan Conley: "Maybe I can help with the orb? I can research."

Veela: "That's a good idea. The Kraleen people were the original inhabitants of this planet, but their civilization is dead. It's about all I know."

Dr. Donovan Conley: "I'll get to it then, see what I can come up with." He stood and smiled. "Thanks for the chat, cap." He stood up from where he was seated, making himself ready to exit her office.

Veela: "Anytime."

#DM-Dr.-Donovan-Conley

Veela: Hey, I'm sorry I didn't get back to you.

Dr. Donovan Conley: No problem. How are you?

Veela: Good. Trying to ignore work.

Dr. Donovan Conley: Me too.

Veela: I thought about you coming to Nashville and all that. I think it'd be alright if we got together for something casual. There's a coffee shop on 21st and Wedgewood. We can meet there.

Dr. Donovan Conley: You'll have to remind me of the place when the time comes. It's still a couple of weeks out.

Veela: Oh, right. I work evenings so if you could do a morning that'd be best.

Dr. Donovan Conley: I might have to sneak out of my work conference for a bit but I'll see what I can do. We'll make something work.

Veela: Sounds good. Keep in touch.

Dr. Donovan Conley: You bet.

———————————

Rachel

———————————

Rachel couldn't believe she'd said yes. Her heart pounded for the next several hours, and she almost forgot to change into the slinky cocktail dress required for her shift at the bar. She hated the way she looked in it. The dress bunched in all the wrong places, though she never received any complaints from the patrons, most of whom were drunk.

She smoothed the dress down as she stood in front of the mirror. Hair curled. Makeup applied. She hadn't forgotten anything while fretting over the coming meet-and-greet with some guy from the internet. An older guy from the internet, at that. What was she getting herself into?

Jenny had no problem with it. She treated the meet-up so casually, but it was a much bigger ordeal for Rachel. It made her uncomfortable to think about some random person invading her personal space.

Though he wasn't random. The men at the bar who would be making comments about her and trying to awkwardly and drunkenly flirt with her were the random ones. It happened every night. Sometimes she even made decent friendships with the respectful men in the bar.

This wouldn't be that bad. First, he wouldn't be drunk if they met for coffee in the morning. Second, it was someone who shared an intellectual passion with her. Even though he hadn't been as knowledgeable in the lore of the books as she was—with her lack of social life, almost no one had as much time to read as she—he tried and had a passion for the game. He seemed pretty intelligent, too, able to quickly get into the role of a space-faring doctor. She'd never doubted his authenticity, which said a lot about his writing ability.

She had to breathe and be calm. It was a couple of weeks away anyway. If she felt uncomfortable, she could always back out.

She had to stop thinking about it and get to work.

Rachel grabbed her keys and her handbag and headed out the door.

Fifteen minutes later, she arrived at work. She slipped through the back door after taking one of the employee parking spaces. Luckily her shift started early enough to where they didn't fill up. Parking on the strip for shifts that began later in the day was terrible.

A band was setting up inside for their next set, one Rachel recognized as Jesse and the Girls, a play on an old eighties song title. Almost all bands down on the strip played the eighties rock songs with a country twang. The tourists found it charming, getting drunk and yelling their anthems, but the same songs set after set, night after night, it was challenging for someone working.

She supposed it could be worse. At least she worked at one of the nicer and cleaner bars. She'd heard horror stories about rats in the kitchen at another place, along with piles of mold and goop from an ancient frier that leaked for years. It was amazing a health inspector hadn't taken them down.

Jenny stood at the main computer to log their orders, cash out checks, and log them in and out of their shifts. The blonde finished logging in and turned to see Rachel with a bright smile.

"Hey," Jenny said.

"What's up?" Rachel asked.

"Living the dream. Gonna be a big tip night; I can feel it."

"Let us pray." Rachel pressed her hands together piously before stepping up to the computer, tapping in her code, and clocking herself in.

Jenny waited so they could walk over to the kitchen together and get their notepads before their table assignments. A Friday night likely would be busy, which meant a big tip night if all went well.

"Did you talk to your online boy?" Jenny asked with a sweet smile.

"I did." Rachel couldn't help but note the blood rushing to her face, making her cheeks hot.

Jenny clicked the top of her pen. "Don't even need to ask; I can tell you've said yes. Good for you. Just relax and have fun with it. Trust me."

Rachel noted the customers making their way inside, the hostess placing them in her section. She had to stop thinking about this, put on a pleasant smile, and have a good night. "We'll see. Time to work."

"Go get 'em."

Space Adventures Online

#Sunflower

□

Aria Benoit: [Comm] "Ship prepped and ready for jump to FTL, captain." The engineer had grease all over her coveralls, but they couldn't see that from her location.

Ray Athan: He sat at the helm station, waiting for the order to come from the captain so they could get out of here.

Veela: "Alright, let's head back to Palmer Station." Veela crossed her arms in front of the captain's chair. "Gun it, Ray."

Lizyin (GM): Before they could jump, a ship appeared on the scanner — an Aryshan vessel.

Lt. Chandler: "Aryshans!" He put the claw-shaped ship on the screen.

Veela: "Shields. Ready weapons. I don't suppose we can still jump out of here?" Veela tensed, gripping the armrests of her captain's chair.

Lizyin (GM): The ship was in their path.

Ray Athan: "No ma'am."

Dr. Donovan Conley: The doctor stood at the back, unsure what he could do in the current situation, so he remained quiet.

Veela: "This isn't good. We aren't a match for an Aryshan ship." ((It's not one of their big warships, is it?))

Lizyin (GM): ((No, scout ship, but still a big threat for a freight vessel like the Sunflower))

Lizyin (GM): You receive a transmission.

Lt. Chandler: "Transmission incoming." He monitored his console.

Veela: "On screen."

Lt. Chandler: He put the image on the screen.

Lizyin (GM): A middle aged Aryshan man appeared wearing their fleet military uniform, silver skin, the crown ridges tall above his head. He had his eyes narrowed and did not appear to be in a mood to negotiate. "You will hand the orb over to us."

Veela: The captain tried to look cool an collected. "I have no idea what you're talking about."

Aryshan (NPC): "Don't toy with us. We can destroy your ship with a shot," the Aryshan said.

Veela: "Cut feed." She turned to Chandler.

Lt. Chandler: He turned off the feed. "What are you thinking?"

Veela: "Well, they're not going to destroy us if they truly believe we have something aboard they want. They have no other real reason to hassle us."

Lt. Chandler: "Which buys us a little time. I'm not sure I can fend off a full ship of Aryshan soldiers by myself."

Dr. Donovan Conley: "I can try to help."

Lt. Chandler: The security officer laughed. "No offense, doc."

Veela: She gave Don a little smirk. "Thank you."

Dr. Donovan Conley: "None taken." He grumbled.

Veela: "We just need to figure out a way to get out of here before they are able to take the orb…or stash it somewhere they can't find it."

Ray Athan: "I have a hidden compartment under the floor in my quarters."

Veela: She snapped her fingers. "Go get the orb and put it there."

Ray Athan: "Aye ma'am." He got up from his station and hustled to the captain's ready room to try to get the orb.

Lizyin (GM): When Ray left his station, you could feel the ship shake as a tractor claw descended from the Aryshan's ship grappled the Sunflower.

Dr. Donovan Conley: He braced himself. "This isn't good.

Lt. Chandler: He tapped his tactical controls. "No, it isn't."

Veela: "Fire on the grappling line. See if you can get us released."

Lt. Chandler: He fired pulse cannons.

Lizyin (GM): The shots fired, but the way the claw was situated it did little good. The Aryshans dragged them closer to the ship and eventually into their docking bay.

8

Jason

Jason reclined his seat as the plane reached a cruising altitude above the clouds. He stared out the window at the puffy white blanket below them, where one would never know from looking at it about the immense world resting underneath. People could be the same, he thought as he tried his best to relax.

It made him nervous.

He should have been thinking about the convention, the people he would meet there, the business contacts and tips he could both impart and receive, but instead, his nerves had him stuck on Rachel. They'd only talked a handful of times, and though there seemed to be some connection there, all she had been was text on a screen. They'd never spoken. He didn't know what she looked like. This was a pure blind meeting.

He'd been on dating apps a few times. It had even resulted in a couple of successful evenings, but those relationships quickly dwindled. Everyone on there liked to present an idealized version of themselves. I like to take long walks on the beach, have deep conversations, and have something real, not just a shallow relationship. People wrote similarly on almost every profile, but at the same time, they seemed to make their decisions almost purely based on looks. It resulted in strange conversations and more awkward and disconnected dates than not.

This was different, though. One, it wasn't necessarily a date. Rachel would just be hanging out with him with no expectations. Yet he couldn't help but be on edge with the whole experience. He wanted her to like him, to not mess up their situation in the game, but beyond that, he hoped this brilliant girl could somehow become a part of his life.

His pale reflection appeared in the window, reminding him of where he was, up in the air, with his own life. Jason tended to overthink matters, which was very useful in many business scenarios where he could use his mental proclivities to game out investments, which worked more often than not. However, relationships only tended to cause problems, especially at the beginning.

Most people wanted to have fun and wanted something light and entertaining. They built a connection from here. Jason intellectually understood this, but he was a man who wanted something for the long term. It was all too easy to find short-term, flighty romances and much more difficult to discover something real.

He sighed to himself, which made his companion in the seat next to him take a look over.

"Is everything all right?" the man asked.

"Yes," Jason replied. "Just nervous about a meeting."

It was true enough. He shouldn't be nervous, though. This wasn't high school, and he'd been around the block enough to both know how to treat a girl right and hopefully build a real connection with her.

His answer seemed to satisfy the man beside him, who promptly leaned his head against the rest again and closed his eyes. Jason wished he could calm his mind and do similarly, but all he could do was to keep staring out the window, wondering how meeting Rachel would turn out.

Space Adventures Online

\#Sunflower

Lizyin (GM): Aryshans popped the hatch into the ship and boarded. A party of five of them entered with their pulse weapons drawn.

Veela: "Get ready to fight off the Aryshans. We need to clear our ship if we're going to get out of here." Veela positioned herself behind the captain's chair, with her gun pointed for when they came through to the bridge.

Lt. Chandler: He kept his weapon trained, off to the side and ready to draw fire.

Ray Athan: He had his gun drawn as well.

Veela: She hit her comm to talk to engineering. "Aria, do you have any ideas on how to get us out of here?"

Aria Benoit: "We have to get rid of their tractor claw somehow. If you can hold them off I'll work on getting charges set where the claws are grappling us." Her voice came through the bridge's speakers.

Veela: "Copy. Sounds good." Veela readied herself to fend off the invasion.

Lizyin (GM): The doors to the bridge hissed and finally burst open. Aryshan soldiers pushing through.

Lt. Chandler: He didn't wait, firing on the first one to enter, using his trained precision as a soldier to strike true.

Ray Athan: From behind the helm station he fired his pulse pistol at the same time.

Veela: Veela also fired, trying to hit one of the targets behind the first one.

Lizyin (GM): Ray and Chandler both hit the same Aryshan, while Veela hit a second beside them. The next three took cover, returning fire at the crew.

Lt. Chandler: Chandler didn't have a place to hide so he just kept at it, trying to pick them off before they did too much damage.

Ray Athan: ((Shouldn't the Doctor be here?))

Veela: ((he's on a plane right now))

Lizyin (GM): ((Should I injure him again? Lol))

Veela: ((Nah. That'd just be mean!))

Ray Athan: He made sure those blasts hit the console and not him before poking his gun out again and pointing toward the corridor for another shot.

Veela: Veela ducked behind the captain's chair. "How many are left?"

Lizyin (GM): A third Aryshan fell to the ground from Chandler's blast. Ray's missed.

Ray Athan: ((I resent this.))

Lizyin (GM): ((Tough cookie.))

Lt. Chandler: "Two more!"

Lizyin (GM): One of the back lines of Aryshans came forward and he tackled Chandler to the ground. His pulse pistol went sliding across the deck. The second shot at the captain's chair, blasting the top of it to bits.

Veela: "My chair!" She returned fire.

Ray Athan: He watched the grapple, unsure if he should take action. He could hit his companion, but then again, he could also end this. He stood, taking careful aim and waited until the Aryshan's back was faced toward him and fired at him.

Lt. Chandler: He struggled on the ground with the aRyshan when he saw Ray firing. "Are you crazy?!"

Lizyin (GM): The two Aryshans crumpled to the floor, and the bridge was safe once again.

Veela: She stood and hit her comm button. "Aria, what's the status down there?"

Aria Benoit: "Charges set and ready to blow, captain."

Veeela: "Set them off."

Aria Benoit: She did so from her engineering station.

Lizyin (GM): The charges detonated around the claw, damaging the hull of the Sunflower in a nonessential area, but releasing them from their clamps.

Veela: "Alright, Ray. Get us out of her hand back to Palmer Station."

Ray Athan: *He slid back up into his pilots seat, glad his console was still intact, and set coordinates before blasting them away from the Aryshan ship and then to FTL.

Lizyin (GM): ((That's a wrap for now, folks.))

Veela: ((Thanks Lizyin))

#DM-Dr.-Donovan-Conley

Veela: You missed a nice wrap-up scene while you were out flying tonight. Sorry everyone decided to go ahead and get to the action without you. Hope you land safely and talk to you soon. I'll give you my number so you don't have to log on to try to talk to me when you're here.

Rachel

Rachel's heart fluttered with both excitement and fear. Her shoulders had tightened, and she noticed herself hunching over at her desk while she looked in her mirror, so she tried to straighten her posture. In fifteen minutes, she would have to go and meet Jason.

Her phone lit up with a text, him letting her know he'd gotten out of his morning business meetings at whatever convention he'd been at, and he would be on his way to the coffee shop soon.

She'd picked the place because it would be far enough away it would be difficult to follow her back home or to her work if there were a problem, but it still made her nervous. Too many what-ifs rolled through her head.

It didn't help to have her apartment so quiet. So she put on some music from Rameses B, a chill electronic artist she'd discovered through a random internet station. The music had a calming and relaxing feel, but not so much that it put her to sleep. She liked to put it on in the background while she role-played, which eventually associated the music with comfort. It was also nice not to listen to blaring 80s or country rock like she did all day at work.

Rachel started to second-guess her choices. She'd put some mild curls in her hair to look more done up, but what if she looked better with straight hair? I was too late to do anything about it now, but she wanted to present her best, despite her fears about how Jason might be in real life.

She applied her makeup to keep her appearance pleasant but not overly fake. She only wore some basic foundation and lipstick which matched the natural tone of her lips, not bothering with eyeliner or anything excessively fancy.

One last look in the mirror, and she would have to go with it. She was going to be late.

She grabbed her things and headed out to her car.

Once at her stall in the garage below her apartment, Rachel hesitated. She could always text him and say she wasn't feeling well, get out of this, and pretend it never happened once she returned to the chat. He wouldn't know any better and be gone by the time she "felt better," which could keep things the way they were.

The game was so wonderful. She had so much fun with this plot line and had her player group, who were all friendly with her, but meeting someone could change all of that. Her dread overcame her as she gripped her door handle, finding it difficult to get a solid hold with her palms sweating.

In reality, she didn't fear him being some creepy weirdo. She had a better sense from talking to him than that. The more frightening prospect of this meet-up would be the consequences if she liked him. Then what would she do?

One day at a time, she told herself. She would have to try to have fun and not worry about it.

Space Adventures Online

#General:

Lizyin (GM): The plot thickens.

Veela: Thanks for running the game, Liz <3. This has been the best plot line yet.

Lizyin (GM): No problem.

Ray Athan: I still think you should have injured the doctor again. Would have been funny.

Veela: We need to injure someone -else- so our esteemed physician can have something to do with his job.

Lt. Chandler: I'm too well-trained in combat to get injured.

Lizyin (GM): Don't tempt me, Chandler.

Lt. Chandler: What?

Ray Athan: Doctor hasn't been on at all since his flight, yeah?

Veela: He's been busy. He said he has a work convention.

Ray Athan: Ahh.

Lt. Chandler: Hopefully he doesn't drop out of the habit of playing. Medics are hard to find.

Veela: They shouldn't be. Doctors almost always have something to do in game.

Lizyin (GM): Most people prefer direct combat roles. Is what it is.

Veela: I guess.

Aria Benoit: I don't think he's quitting. He seems pretty excited about the game.

Lt. Chandler: Just speculating. Don't mind me. I'm in a mood.

Aria Benoit: Everything okay?

Lt. Chandler: Yeah, I'll be fine. Thanks.

Ray Athan: Don't go getting emo on us, security guy. You're supposed to be the tough one.

Lt. Chandler: hahah, in character maybe.

Veela: We're here for you if you ever need to talk.

Lt. Chandler: Thanks, Veela. I try to keep my real life separate from the game, as you know.

Ray Athan: You never stop reminding us.

#DM-Ray-Athan

Ray Athan: Hey.

Veela: Sup

Ray Athan: Was a fun event in game.

Veela: Yeah, it was.

Ray Athan: I'm just bored waiting for work to end.

Veela: I'm actually sitting in a coffee shop waiting for Conley to arrive.

Ray Athan: The doctor?

Veela: The same one.

Ray Athan: Wow, he moves fast. Didn't you say it was a work convention?

Veela: Yeah. It just happens to be here. lol, what do you mean moves fast?

Ray Athan: He was just asking about you a couple of weeks ago. He's into you even though he's trying to be coy about it. Pretty lame if you ask me. I was like, just talk to the girl.

Veela: Huh, interesting.

Ray Athan: You'll have to let me know how it goes.

Veela: I will. I'm sure it'll be fine. He seems like a nicc guy.

Ray Athan: Yeah. He's alright.

Veela: There's someone spinning around the coffee shop like he's looking for someone and lost. I think it might be him. I don't know what he looks like. I gotta go. Talk to you later.

Ray Athan: If you need me to call the cops, let me know haha.

Veela: Gee, Lol, I'd thought of that already and got my real life friend on speed dial. Thanks. Later!

9

Jason

When he entered the coffee shop, Jason realized he should have gotten a picture or at least a description of Rachel first. What had he been thinking? This made for an awkward situation as they would have to find each other.

He moved into the line for the register, almost by default, as people tended to migrate in that direction when making their orders first. After the mornings' talks, he could use a little caffeinated pick-me-up.

For the first time since Jason could remember, he spent the morning fretting over what he would wear. He'd gotten so used to doing business online from the comfort of his computer that he could wear whatever he wanted—which in the heat of Nevada's summers typically meant shorts and an old t-shirt. He wasn't trying to impress anyone. It had been years since he'd had to wear a suit and tie or anything of the sort.

Jason went with what he considered a happy medium for a meeting like this. He wore a trim-fitting dark polo, which fit snugly around his arms. It was one of the few polos he liked and thought he looked particularly good in.

He wore jeans to compliment it, a dark blue pair. It seemed simple attire, but he had spent too long debating over various garments before settling on them.

It was too late to change his mind now, even if he would have wanted to. He spun around a couple of times in the coffee shop, trying to see if he could spot anyone who could conceivably be Rachel. She was in her early-to-mid twenties; he knew that much. That matched about thirty percent of the people lingering in or around the coffee shop. Of course, this was a college town, so most of the people would be a little younger.

A panicked thought crossed his mind—what if she decided to back out? Or what if she saw him and decided she wouldn't say anything?

With him turning around looking for someone, it felt like most of the eyes were on him in the coffee shop, which shouldn't have made him uncomfortable, and it was ridiculous to think, but he couldn't help the self-consciousness creeping up his spine. His stomach filled with butterflies. He hadn't felt like this since...

Since he had first gone out with Danielle. She was the last thing he needed to be thinking about now.

One girl with blonde hair and light curls, sat at a table, glancing around the shop in between, looking around at her phone. It had to have been her. But before Jason could make any contact, it was his turn to place an order.

"How can I help you?" The barista asked. She was a young girl with black hair, one light pink streak, tattoos, and a nose ring. For a moment, Jason considered that this might be Rachel's workplace before he saw the name tag said Veronica.

"Ah." He wasn't prepared, looking up at the sign behind her even though he knew full well his coffee order. "Nonfat latte, please. Small."

"Three sixty-five," the girl said.

Jason gave her his credit card, they completed the transaction, and he waited for his coffee. While he did, he meandered over to the table with the blonde. She looked up at him and caught his eye right before he arrived.

"Rachel?" he asked, hopeful.

Her blue eyes shone at him, and God, they were beautiful. She had an innocence to her, something deep and real behind those eyes he didn't see in many people. He wanted to melt right into them.

"Yeah. Jason?" she asked. Her voice had a high-pitched tone, but it was very soft and sweet. It matched her appearance's softness, and Jason instantly knew he liked her.

"That's me." Jason smiled warmly before motioning to the chair across from her. "May I?"

"Sure, go a—"

Jason!" The barista called over from the bartop. He pushed Jason's latte to the edge of the counter.

"Hold that thought," Jason said, turning and scooting through the line to get to the end of the bar, grab his drink, and head back over to her.

Rachel looked nervous, which was understandable. She kept touching her phone as if it was her one anchor keeping her safe. He would have to put her at ease, or this would be one awkward talk.

Jason helped himself to the seat, glancing down at the latte. The barista had made a heart shape with the milk foam atop the light brown espresso color. It was cute and the mark of a coffee maker who cared, or at least the establishment made them pretend to care. Either way, he liked the place and sipped the coffee.

It was the perfect balance of flavor without bitterness. Much better than the corporate chains he frequented when in a hurry, which seemed too often these days.

But he didn't care about the coffee. He was here for Rachel, and she was looking at him expectantly. He'd have to lead the conversation somehow.

"I picked up the books finally and read the first one on the way here." He probably should have asked about her or her life, but the game and the science fiction series it was based upon was the first thing that came to his mind. He'd spent more time talking to her as her character Veela than her real persona. It made him more comfortable to talk about their shared hobby.

It made her more comfortable too. Her eyes twinkled at the talk of the book. "Oh yeah? What did you think?"

"It was fun. A lot of romance for what I expected to be more of a shoot 'em up." Jason realized he was smiling again, but he didn't want to make himself seem like he was being fake with her, so he tried to drop it. However, something about how Rachel looked when she spoke of the books made him so happy. She had a pure joy for these, and it was adorable.

She laughed. "Yeah. It's interesting to think of what a human and a human-like alien would do in a romantic situation. How would it work? There are bound to be complications. Even more than, uh, it is in real life."

"And it's hard enough already."

Her eyes shifted away from him, creating an awkward pause in the conversation. There were better topics to start on when getting to know someone for the first time. The silent moment made for a lot of tension, something he wanted to undo and return to an excellent, casual topic. God, he didn't want to screw this up.

She was a lot prettier than he had expected her to be. He hadn't known what to expect, to be honest, but she had an air of innocence around her which made it difficult to stop his heart from pounding. This was supposed to be something simple and light, only coffee. He had to remember that.

"Well, it was a lot of fun anyway. I'm excited for the next one," Jason finally said.

Rachel met his eyes again. "Oh, yeah. They only get better. I won't spoil it because there's some interesting complications that pop up you might not be thinking of."

"Cool." Jason took another sip of his latte, trying to think of the next topic, but Rachel hadn't finished with this one.

"Who was your favorite character?"

Jason had to think of it. They were very different in temperaments. "Tol, I think. He has a sort of sense of wonder to him, like everything is new and exciting. I like that feeling."

"Me too," Rachel said. "Both the feeling and favorite character."

"How'd you get involved in the roleplaying? It's kind of a niche thing."

Rachel sucked in her bottom lip before responding. It was cute—everything she did just made him like her more.

"I don't know. I started googling the books and found this on a page's comments. Fell down the rabbit hole," Rachel said.

"Crazy. I was looking for games. It wasn't exactly what I had in mind, but it worked."

"You're having fun then?"

"Yeah, totally. Thanks for including me." Their eyes met again before Rachel looked to the side and down. She had a little insecurity about her, and Jason couldn't see why. He wanted to tell her she was amazing and beautiful and shouldn't be nervous. But he couldn't bring himself to be so direct. Not yet.

"No problem. You're a good role-player. I like writing with you."

"I like writing with you too."

Another pause. Why was it so hard to talk? He needed to calm himself down. He hobnobbed with wealthy investors every day. This conversation should have been easy, in theory. But something about her broke his mind to where he felt like a teenager again, nervously talking to his first crush.

"What do you do exactly for work?" Rachel asked.

"I manage investments. Stocks, bonds, gold, crypto. All sorts of stuff. Sometimes it gets bizarre, and they want me to look into bottling factories for beer companies. It can be challenging but fun too."

"Sounds stressful."

"It can be. I've had a good run of luck, though. Most of what I've done has turned out pretty solid."

"That's good." She shook her head as if something bothered her.

"Something wrong?" Jason cocked his head to the side. If there were, he would do anything to fix it for her.

"Just life stuff. I'm stuck as a waitress even though I have a degree where I should be working with diplomats or corporate boards worldwide. I feel like I'm wasting myself." A slight frown crossed her face.

Seeing her unhappy broke his heart. Jason would have done anything for her to get her to smile. He wasn't sure if he could help, but he would certainly try. "What are you looking to do exactly?"

"International relations of some sort."

"Hmm, you need someone who does business all over the world then," Jason said.

"Yeah. My parents are not exactly connected in big

business. My dad was an airline pilot, and my mom stayed at home. They're retired now." She shrugged.

What could he do here? He could ask around his clients and see if they had anything. But he'd been in this business long enough to know that he couldn't make any promises unless he had a tangible way to deliver. Getting someone's hopes up and then giving them disappointment was a surefire way to disaster. With Rachel, he only wanted to be able to give her positive news. He kept his mouth shut on the matter for now, though he filed away a thought to start poking his clients later.

"I'm sure something will work out for you. It just takes patience, sometimes." Good enough advice. He needed to take it himself before he gushed, confessed his love to her, and moved too fast. She was a catch and didn't know it, and he didn't want to scare her away.

"Thanks. I'm sorry to be a downer. Let's talk about something else, hmm?"

Jason chuckled. "Sure. What do you want to discuss?"

They moved on to telling their life stories. She seemed to have a good family and upbringing, full of love and concern for her from her parents. He felt like he had a similar experience with his parents and even his brother, whom he could tolerate occasionally. It made him miss his family. He'd have to visit them at some point when he got back.

The conversation moved much more smoothly from there. Talk of high school, which they both hated and college, which they both loved; it was easier once they had broken the ice. It made him lose track of the time.

Soon enough, his phone lit up with texts from the guys at the convention. They were heading out to the Nashville strip and wanted him there. As much as he wanted to stay with Rachel, he had a purpose to be out here, which wasn't her. The thought of leaving twisted at his heart.

"I'm sorry, but I think I need to get going," Jason said.

"Oh yeah, your convention. Have fun." Rachel brandished a small smile at him, as innocent and beautiful as the rest of her.

"Thanks. It was great meeting you."

They stood together, and Jason leaned in to give her a soft hug. It wasn't as close or tight as he would have given anything for at that moment, but it was something. Her scent was as wonderful as her touch, a soft but floral nature to her hair. It filled him with such joy he felt like gravity wouldn't hold him down any longer.

"Stay safe. Chat soon?" She asked.

"Yes, captain."

They both laughed as they departed.

Space Adventures Online

#DM-Ray-Athan

———

Ray-Athan: Yo, how'd your little meeting with Veela go?

Dr. Donovan Conley: Really well, I think.

Ray Athan: Deets?

Dr. Donovan Conley: Honestly, she's amazing. I can't believe how smart she is.

Ray Athan: Well, duh. I could have told you that. You've seen how she writes a space captain. Not many girls can do that.

Dr. Donovan Conley: It's different in person than writing with someone. I didn't even know how I'd expected her to be. I'd never even heard her voice before.

Ray Athan: So what are you gonna do now?

Dr. Donovan Conley: I have no idea. I live halfway across the country so it can't really work out, which upsets me. But I still want to pursue her. It's all I'm thinking about, can't even focus on my work conference.

Ray Athan: LMAO, okay.

Dr. Donovan Conley: What do you think I should do?

Ray Athan: Not be a simp.

Dr. Donovan Conley: I'm trying to be serious.

Ray Athan: I don't know, man. If you really like her just be honest and see where it goes?

Dr. Donovan Conley: Okay. I'll try

―――

#Palmer-Station:

―――

Veela: Once they arrived back at the station, Veela walked toward Green Sector again, where the alien species congregated on the station. She felt like all eyes are on her, glancing around in a paranoid fashion. One thing was for certain, she didn't want to risk any Aryshan entanglements.

Lt. Chandler: Chandler followed along with his captain, looking menacing and tough as he could.

Veela: Eventually they made their way into the alien bar they had been in earlier. She approached the bartender and asked after Jorin Issim.

Bartender (NPC): "Are you certain you want him? He's in a hot mess with the authorities, I hear." The bartender scrutinized her as if she were crazy.

Veela: "Isn't he supposed to be part of some archeological guild from the government?" Now she became very concerned about this orb and exactly what it could do. Was she in danger? Veela slid a credit chit across the bar toward the tender to give him some incentive.

Bartender (NPC): "I don't ask about my patrons' personal lives too closely as a rule. Guild or thief, I don't know. You seem like a nice girl though, so I'll give you what I know. I hear here's holding out in the slum quarters in D-131. You can try there. But don't tell him I sent you." He went back to making his drinks, acting as if she had never been there and he hadn't seen her right in front of him.

Veela: "Thank you." She walked away from the bar and back to Chandler.

Lt. Chandler: "Any luck?"

Veela: "Maybe. A location fo where our contact might be. Let's go." They walked along to the D-sector to try to go find the quarters.

Lizyin (GM): A bunch of seedy humans and aliens lingered around, many seeming on drugs or like they were mentally ill. The hallways seemed cluttered, not cleaned like the majority of the station. This was a small sector where the bad wa overlooked, much like homeless encampments in modern times.

Lt. Chandler: "Stay close. I don't want you to get hurt." Chandler kept his hand close to his pulse pistol.

Veela: They continued along, looking at the markings on the door until they came to 137. Veela didn't feel safe here, but she had to see it through.

Lizyin (GM): They arrived without incident.

Veela: She looked at the door with the marking on it, letting out a deep breath from her nerves before finally ringing the chime to see if they were there.

Lt. Chandler: He kept his eyes peeled to make sure no one was going to ambush them from either side of the corridor.

Lizyin (GM): The room opened to a smoky mist with the lights off inside. "Come, come!" A voice said.

Veela: She walked into the room, looking for Jorin Issim.

Lizyin (GM): He was there inside the room, the voice

that spoke to her. He looked up when she entered, seated on a chair in the back. "You have the orb?"

Veela: "Perhaps." She stiffened, keeping her eyes peeled for trouble.

Lizyin: (GM): A couple of figures came out of the shadows, both with pulse pistols in hand.

Lt. Chandler: He drew his weapon, pointing at one of the figures. "Drop it."

Lizyin (GM): "It's no matter." Jorin said. "Give me the orb."

Veela: "I didn't bring it because I'm not an idiot. Transfer the credits to my account." Lizyin stood her ground and didn't seem concerned about the mooks with guns.

Lizyin (GM): Jorin motioned his guards back and they complied. "A tough bargain, but I agree. I'll deposit the credits."

Veela: "What's so special about this orb anyway?"

Lizyin (GM): "It's said to be able to have the ability to displace someone in time. The ultimate weapon. The ability to rewrite history." Jorin seemed very eager to get his hands on it. "Or maybe just mistakes one made in the past."

Veela: "Okay. You have my information. We'll be back with it. Come on." Veela turned and left the room.

Lt. Chandler: Chandler followed behind, confused as to why this transpired like this.

Rachel

Rachel flopped down into the driver's seat of her car and let out a deep exhale. That had been one of the most nerve-wracking experiences of her life. Why had meeting Jason been so much of a difficulty for her? It was just coffee with a friend. At least, she thought he was a friend. But how he looked at her pierced right through to her soul.

Maybe that was why she had been so on edge. His gaze had such intensity; it was far beyond what she typically experienced with the guys leering at her at the bar every evening. That she could deal with, but he seemed genuinely interested in her. It was different.

As she stared at the black leather of her dashboard, Rachel realized she liked it. She wished she could be back there again, talking to him, having him listen to her talk about her life's experiences. He was a man who cared.

Or was it just an act? She'd been on dates before where a man pretended to listen to her, only to act later as if he'd never heard a single word she'd uttered. It was more than annoying, but it didn't seem like that was the case with Jason.

He was different. Maybe it was because of the game. Someone with a geeky interest like Space Adventures Online couldn't play some cool, sophisticated game. She already knew he had a hobby and a habit far lamer than any guy would admit on a first, second, or even third date. Heck, Rachel never told people about her online roleplaying. How could she?

It embarrassed her to think about it, but she would never have met Jason without the game.

The only question was—now what? Jason lived across the country. He had a life, a job, and she barely knew anything about him besides what she'd learned in a cursory talk. She shouldn't worry about it because she would probably never meet him again.

Her phone buzzed, snapping her from her thoughts. Rachel dug into her handbag and pulled it out. Jenny.

Sup Rach? How did it go?

Rachel flicked past the home screen to get into her texts.

I think really well. He's different. I don't know.

Want to come over and talk about it?

Yeah.

It was what she needed. Jenny was someone she could talk to and trust with anything. She had experience with relationships like no one else. Most ended quickly, but it was much more than Rachel had in recent months. She hadn't had a real relationship since college, which had split in junior year. It had been a nasty breakup, with the guy going psycho and banging on her door in the early morning hours, even weeks after they'd called it quits. She'd had to call the cops to get him to leave.

Since then, Rachel focused on her school work, hoping it would lead to something—another dead end.

Her heart sank, thinking of all the misfires in her life.

She was overthinking everything now based on one meeting with a man in a coffee shop. Someone she barely knew. She had to breathe and take this one moment at a time, not worry about the future.

Rachel hit the push-button starter to her car and backed out of her parking space. A couple of songs' worth of a drive later, she arrived at Jenny's apartment complex. At this time of day, it was easy to find parking out front. She locked her car and walked toward the apartment.

The place was a little newer than Rachel's, a modern complex with a lot of fake amenities no one used. It sounded good upon signing a lease deal, but Rachel found having a cheaper apartment was better for the long run than living somewhere like this.

She reached Jenny's unit, a place on the first floor, and knocked on the door.

Jenny opened the door a moment later, motioning Rachel to come in. She had a mirror hanging on the entryway wall and a rack to hold a few different choices of handbags and coats.

It was a studio with a little kitchenette attached to a bedroom. Not much for entertaining, but Jenny was the type to go out rather than stay home anyway, so it fit her. Clothes littered the floor, with Jenny not keeping the place spectacularly clean, but it didn't feel dirty either.

"Tell me about him," Jenny said. "Want a coke or something?"

"I'm good," Rachel said. There was a small bar area with a couple of stools, so she sat on one. Jenny took a seat on the other. "I don't know. It was really intense like he had a real interest in my life. I don't know why."

"Was he cute?"

"I wasn't thinking about that."

Jenny laughed. "If you've got chemistry, you'd say yes."

"Okay, yes, he wasn't bad looking by any means."

"But you didn't feel the fire."

"I don't know. I don't do things like you. I like a slow burn." She hated using the fire analogy, but it worked well enough.

"I see." As she leaned her elbow on the bar, Jenny sounded almost like a therapist. "So, you like him."

Rachel looked down at her shoes momentarily, unsure what she should say to such a comment. She didn't move that fast. She wanted to get to know someone better before making such a determination. But she couldn't help but admit there was a little feeling there. He was sweet, and he was smart. It counted for something, but she didn't know what it meant for the long run. "Yeah, I guess so."

Jenny looked overjoyed, leaning in to give her a small hug. "That's great! I'm excited for you."

Rachel didn't feel great. She felt confused more than anything else. "What am I supposed to do now?'

Jenny shrugged. "You hope he calls you again."

Space Adventures Online

#Sunflower

Veela: Veela hustled back into her ship, closing the door behind her when she entered, making sure no one could follow her and her crew.

Lt. Chandler: "You look nervous." Chandler walked along with her.

Ray Athan: "Of course she does. That dealer, or whatever he is, was giving shady vibes." Ray shook his head. "I thought he was a government type like you, Chandler. Unless you're hiding something too."

Lt. Chandler: He scoffed at Ray.

Veela: "What do you mean?"

Ray Athan: "The way Jorin was so adamant about getting this, there's something more to it. This orb, I don't know. Obviously he wants to go back in time and fix something of his own. It's brought us trouble. Aryshans, and who knows what he'll do?"

Veela: "I've been thinking the same thing. I want to bring it to an archaeologist friend of mine and see if he can't make heads or tails of it.

Dr. Donovan Conley: He stepped onto the main bridge from his little medical bay to see everyone gathering there. "Hey. What'd I miss?"

Veela: "Donovan." She smiled when she said his name.

Dr. Donovan Conley: He smiled right back at her. It was nice to see the captain's face again.

Ray Athan: "Always best to have a doctor and not need him. How you doin', doc?"

Dr. Donovan Conley: "Not so bad. Maybe a little bored, but there's plenty of things to read."

Veela: "We were just discussing the orb we picked up and what to do with it. I think we're going to keep it and try to talk to an archeologist friend of mine to get more information. Sorry if you were hoping for a quick payday."

Ray Athan: "You didn't ask us that question." He smirked.

Veela: She grinned at Ray. "You're more replaceable than our medic."

Ray Athan: "Hey!"

Lt. Chandler: He only chuckled at the interchange.

Veela: "Kidding aside, I think this is a far bigger deal than just a quick payday. We should check it out. Let's set a course to the Dative system. My archeological contact is at the colony there." She spoke decisively with command.

Dr. Donovan Conley: He was glad this wasn't going to be just a quick assignment and have to find another job and move on. It had been fairly easy so far, which he hoped would keep up.

Aria Benoit: "Engine room ready." She spoke through the comm system, listening to everything goin on up above. "And I'm all in for a good adventure."

Veela: "Then let's get going. Mr. Athan, call the docking authority and tell them we'd like to depart."

Ray Athan: He moved to sit down at the conn and

opened up a line to the station. "Sunflower here. Request departure."

GM (Lizyin): "Palmer Station copy that. You are cleared to depart as soon as the bay doors open." The bay cleared and the door opened soon afterward.

Veela: She watched as the ship pulled out of the docking bay and back into space. They would jump to FTL soon and be back on their way.

Dr. Donovan Conley: He watched along with the captain, but he couldn't help but hope this would last a little longer. He thought of something, and decided to take a risk. "Captain?"

Veela: "Yes, doctor?"

Dr. Donovan Conley: "I picked up a bottle of aged whiskey on the station. Would you like to share a glass with me?"

Veela: She turned back to him, eyes shining brightly toward him. "I'd be delighted to."

Dr. Donovan Conley: "To my quarters then?"

Veela: She laughed. "No. Mine. Captain's prerogative to have the nicest and largest room on the ship."

10

Jason

After the day's events and talk on the markets, Jason went to the bar with a group of financial advisors. Tim was with him, along with a friend of his—Tony, from New York. Tony was a skinny, tall man from Cuba. He had a look to him which made him look ambiguous as to his descent, light tan skin, but curly black hair. He was energetic and loved to drink, but then, they all did.

The hotel bar was modern chic, with a metal bar, a big open ceiling with vents and lighting rigs showing, and shelves made of glass to highlight the top shelf bottles. The sound of soft electronica music sounded in the background, along with the constant sound of ice against metal from the martini shakers.

Jason's crew had gotten there in time to get a couch by the window, drinks piling all over the glass coffee table in front of them. The place was alive with conversations of dozens of people, Jason's people included. However, Jason wasn't paying attention. He kept looking at his phone, opening the Space Adventures Online chatroom. He could hardly concentrate on anything since meeting Rachel. The business talks during the day had all but flown past.

She hadn't been online since their role-play last evening, and she hadn't sent him any direct messages, which had him worried she possibly hadn't enjoyed their coffee experience as much as he had. It seemed like they had a deep connection; did she not feel the same way?

Nervous butterflies filled his stomach, even more than when he had gone to meet her. Now they had interacted in real life; he'd seen how beautiful she was both as a person and in her appearance; it felt so different to him. It was real when it had just been text on a screen a few hours prior.

"Hey, you gonna join the conversation?" Tim asked, smacking Jason in the arm.

Jason looked up from his phone with a sheepish smile. "Sorry about that."

"Game going on or something?" Tim asked about sports, but Jason didn't follow much until the playoffs. It was fun to get in on the championship excitement, but getting too invested in a team was hard when one was from Reno. They didn't have any sports teams, and he couldn't justify cheering for Las Vegas nor his old hometown of L.A. He'd abandoned the place, after all.

"Nah, just looking at texts."

"Ah. The girl you were talking about at our last lunch."

"You got me." Jason slid his phone back into his pocket.

"Didn't you say she was from here? Why don't you have her come down to the bar?"

The idea didn't seem too bad, but Jason didn't want to involve Rachel with a group of guys. It was too soon. He'd hardly gotten to know her at all. It would be overwhelming for the girl and could go sideways too easily. "Nah. I already got lunch with her yesterday."

"How'd that go?" Tim asked. The others seemed to be off in their conversations without them.

"Good, I think. We have a solid connection. She's smart."

"Well, you only live once, Jas. If she's out here, you gotta make the move." Tim shrugged and turned the topic of conversation to baseball with Tony. They cared about sports, playing in fantasy leagues with as much data analysis as their day jobs—perhaps more. Jason never understood why someone would want to do for fun what they did for work, but he supposed if they were good at it and enjoyed it, it made some sense.

Tim might have been right about only living once, though. As much as he would have typically had fun at the bar with the group of guys, he wanted to be elsewhere—and that was with Rachel. Bringing her out with them would have been a bad idea, but maybe he could go somewhere with her.

He slid out from his seat at the end of the booth. "If you'll excuse me, guys. I think I'm going to call it early."

"So soon?" Tony said. "We were talking about going down to the strip in a bit and catch some bands."

"Don't worry about it," Tim said. "He's gonna go out, just not with us." Laughter followed, the men going back to their good time.

They'd be fine without him, but Jason felt self-conscious going on Space Adventures Online with everyone else around. It was the only way he'd be able to talk to Rachel, though. With the bar as lively as ever, Jason slipped out and returned to his hotel room.

Space Adventures Online

#Sunflower

Veela: Veela had a larger quarters than the rest of the crew, with a formal dining table, a nice seating area, and a secondary bedroom behind closed doors. It made for a rather comfortable space with one wall having a view of the stars beyond. She tidied up the place, waiting for her company.

Dr. Donovan Conley: Donovan rang the chime from outside.

Veela: "Come in." She stepped toward the door.

Dr. Donovan Conley: The door opened to allow him in. Donovan dressed in business casual attire, holding a bottle of whiskey as he'd promised. "Hey."

Veela: She looked up at him, eyes twinkling. "Hi. This stuff any good?"

Dr. Donovan Conley: "I'll have to let you be the judge, captain." As he stepped further inside, the doors closed behind him.

Veela: "You can call me Veela." She kept her voice quiet, a change from her usual commanding tone.

Dr. Donovan Conley: "And you can call me Don." He set the bottle down on the table.

Veela: She moved to a cupboard and retrieved two glasses. "Ice?"

Dr. Donovan Conley: "I like mine neat."

Veela: She retrieved ice for herself and left his glass empty before setting both on the table. Then, she took a seat, motioning to one next to her.

Dr. Donovan Conley: He followed, before popping the bottle of whiskey and pouring them both a generous amount into the glasses. "It's got a smoky flavor to it, my preferred taste."

Veela: She swirled her glass around, looking at the amber liquid before bringing it to her lips. She enjoyed the taste. "Not bad."

Dr. Donovan Conley: He couldn't help but follow the way she moved the glass to her lips. It certainly made him thirsty. He raised his own glass to her. "To a crazy adventure."

Veela: She clinked her glass against his. "You got that right. I hope this is the right call."

Dr. Donovan Conley: "I'm sure it will be. You're a natural leader."

Veela: She flushed a little at the compliment. "Thanks. You're not so bad yourself, Don."

Dr. Donovan Conley: His eyes met hers firmly, heart pounding. They were alone together and drinking. A recipe for throwing inhibitions out the window. She was beautiful, her Eternite features exotic compared to those of regular humans. He found himself leaning in closer to her.

Veela: She found herself compelled by the doctor, leaning in closer as well.

Dr. Donovan Conley: He brought his lips to hers, giving her a soft kiss.

Veela: Veela allowed him to kiss her, but then pulled back. "I'm not sure I should be fraternizing with the crew like this."

Dr. Donovan Conley: "I think it's a little late for that." He gave her a wam smile.

Veela: She laughed. "Perhaps it is."

Dr. Donovan Conley: He took her by the hand, entwining her fingers with his and tugged her toward him.

Veela: She wordlessly let herself up and slip into his lap. "Why, doctor. Is it time for an examination?"

Dr. Donovan Conley: He laughed along with her, and kissed her again, harder this time, pulling her body against hers.

Veela: ((FTB time))

Dr. Donovan Conley: ((FTB?))

Veela: ((Fade to black. We stop scenes like this cuz we don't always know what age people are and we don't want anything inappropriate in the server. Just assume what happens happens.))

Dr. Donovan Conley: ((Sounds good. Thanks for playing.))

#DM-Veela

Dr. Donovan Conley: Rachel.

Veela: Sup?

Dr. Donovan Conley: I'm up in my hotel room thinking. This is my last night here and I really would like to see you again. Do you want to go out?

Veela: It's pretty late already.

Dr. Donovan Conley: Nashville doesn't get popping til 10:30 anyway.

Veela: But I work.

Dr. Donovan Conley: Alright, if you don't want to.

Veela: I didn't say I don't want to.

Dr. Donovan Conley: Women are confusing.

Veela: Shut up. I'm thinking.

Dr. Donovan Conley: Ok.

Veela: I'm tired, but I'm considering it.

Dr. Donovan Conley: What if it's the last time we can ever be together?

Veela: Alright. Sappy. Fine, fine. I'll go out. How about the RoundUp Saloon in 20 minutes?

Dr. Donovan Conley: I don't know what that is, but I can find it.

Veela: Sounds good. I'll see you then.

Dr. Donovan Conley: Later.

Rachel

What was she thinking? It was late; she'd been off work for a few hours already, her hair looked like a train wreck, and she didn't even give herself time to do much other than briefly reapply her makeup before heading out the door.

The streets downtown were busy, as they often were on a Saturday night. Rachel would be lucky to find parking anywhere near the strip, which would make her late. With Jason, he'd probably catch a ride share down here for a walk from wherever his hotel was and not have to deal with it. She probably should have taken a ride also, but Rachel didn't have the thirty or forty dollars to spare when she was trying to pinch pennies.

Eventually, she found a paid parking space, which cost ten dollars for the night, making Rachel mumble that she probably should have just taken a rideshare after all, but she looked at the time it would take on the app, and with parking, she'd been at twenty minutes on the dot. She had to hurry so Jason wouldn't wait too long.

She traversed the streets of Nashville alone, groups out drinking already, with a few homeless scattered in trying to panhandle. Musicians busked in the streets, and the cars moved slowly down the strip as tourists tried to get a good look at the nightlife the city was so famous for.

Eventually, Rachel made it to the RoundUp, an old wooden facade built onto a three-story building, with a bar on each floor and a band playing on each one at this time of night. There was a small line out front of people waiting to get in, with a bouncer checking the I.D.s of the patrons. Rachel was all too aware of how many underage drinkers tried to sneak into the various bars.

Jason stood out front, wearing a collared shirt and jeans, casual yet classy enough. He looked at his phone, leaning against the building.

Rachel approached him. "Jason?"

He looked up at her, fumbling with his phone and sliding it back into his pocket. "Oh, hey, Rachel. Thanks for coming out on such short notice."

She gave him a small smile, happy to see him again. "It sounded like fun."

His attention turned to the bar behind him as the first-floor band started a Guns 'n Roses song. "This is your hangout, then?"

"Not really. I try not to go to the strip when I'm off work," Rachel said.

They filtered into the entrance line. "Is this where you work then?"

Rachel shook her head. She didn't invite him to her work because she didn't want to spend her off hours there. Even though most of these bars on the strip were the same to her, including the RoundUp, it still didn't have the oppressive feeling of showing up at one's job. She could only imagine what Chris would say if she'd brought a date there.

Rachel flushed in the face as she realized she considered this a date.

"No," Rachel said. "I don't want to go back to work. We'd get pestered by my manager; it wouldn't be very fun at all. It's mostly the same, though. People always say they have their favorite bars, but they're mostly all the same out here." She shrugged. "It's for tourists, really."

Jason frowned. "Well, I don't want to have to act like a tourist. If you prefer—"

"No, it's fine. I don't get out much at all, to be honest. I just work and play the game, you know?" Rachel didn't want to make him feel self-conscious. She already felt awkward, unsure how to proceed or what to do.

"Me too. I used to be a partier back in my college days, but in the past couple of years, I've just had no desire to go out anymore."

"What happened?"

His frown deepened. Whatever problem he had, it made Jason uncomfortable. His eyes drifted away from her, down to the table and the Q.R. code menu taped to it for people to use their phoniest look at a cocktail list.

Rachel hoped this wouldn't ruin his night. Maybe she'd pressed too far into his personal business for their second meeting. She'd never been good in these situations or had much experience with them. "I'm sorry," she said.

"No, it's fine." He tried to force a smile but looked at her with uncertainty. "I probably shouldn't be telling you this on an early date, but I guess I might as well. I was engaged. We were heavy into drinking, parties, and shows. We pushed it to our limits and got up for work the next morning. That lifestyle just led to trouble, and, well, I got drunk one night, brought home a girl had a long conversation with her and she kissed me. I was stupid and young. It's not something I'm proud of."

"Oh," Rachel said. She had to agree it didn't give her the warm and fuzzies about him, but she did appreciate him being honest. At least he was open with her. That was good, wasn't it?

"We'd just agreed to move out to Nevada too. I bought a nice big house, something I'd always dreamed of having but couldn't afford in California with the housing prices there… and that was it. So now I live in a big house alone."

"That's a pretty heavy story," Rachel said, unable to help but exhaling a long sigh.

"It is. I'm sorry. I hope it doesn't kill the mood too much." He slid his hand across the table, inviting her to take it.

It left him vulnerable if she declined, and she couldn't say she was in much of a mood for a touch, but something about him. Rachel liked him, and she appreciated his honesty. She took his hand. His fingers were warm, filling her with comfort. She hadn't touched someone like this since college, and it felt so good.

"I've never been the best at relationships either," Rachel said. "I'm better online. You can think about your responses that way."

"I'd never thought of that. Most of my work is online. It's probably very similar to how I deal with people."

Rachel noted the band taking a break and finishing their set, the lights going up in the room, and house music coming through the speakers. She turned back to him. "You can pretty much work anywhere with that setup, yeah?"

Jason's brow furrowed as he considered. "I suppose so. I'd never really thought of it before. I just fell into a routine and stayed where I was at."

Did it seem too forward of her? It sounded now like

she had invited him to move to Nashville to be with her. Rachel wasn't sure she wanted that. She'd just met him, but the words had escaped anyway. Her cheeks flushed hot with embarrassment. "Oh."

"Is something the matter?" He looked perplexed. "I've ruined it by telling you my past, huh?"

"No, no. Not at all. I'm having a good time." The situation had turned awkward, and Rachel had to figure out a way to get it back to normal, if possible. "Maybe we should close up and go for a walk down the strip?"

"Not a bad idea." Jason waved his hand to get the tab. He handed the waitress his credit card and paid for everything.

Once Jason had paid, they headed out the doors to the bar, making their way down the street. It didn't matter what night it was on the strip; tourists littered the street. A roving party bus blasted music. A bachelorette party made far too much noise while stumbling in their matching t-shirts, and a man stood in the street with a guitar singing country tunes with an open guitar case to try to get tips. For some, it provided a novel experience, but for a local like Rachel, she found the whole scene distasteful and anything but romantic.

Still, her heart fluttered when Jason took her hand, entwining his fingers with hers for a walk down the street. They didn't say anything for a long while. He seemed to enjoy the scenery and the people watching, even if Rachel had little interest in it. She didn't complain, not wanting to ruin his time.

After a while, Jason stopped and turned toward her. "I like you."

Rachel stifled a breath from the admission. It had been obvious. He'd been trying to touch her all night, leaning in close, trying to impress her as best he could. But this didn't feel like the other times men had wanted to pick her up in the bars. Instead, he seemed sincere, like he didn't do this every day. She looked up at him, filled with warmth from the admission. "I like you too."

Jason took it as a sign and bent in to kiss her. Rachel instinctively flinched, not having been in a position like this for a long time. It gave him pause as he looked at her questioningly.

"It's okay," she breathed.

He completed the kiss, his lips touching hers. He had the perfect mix of gentleness and firmness to the kiss. She felt her lips part as his tongue found hers. Rachel couldn't help but melt into him, the warmth turning into a burning fire. He wrapped his arms around her, and she closed her eyes.

Space Adventures Online

#Daltive-IV

GM (Lizyin): The Sunflower dropped out of FTL in the Daltive system. It had seven planets, one of which was very large and had a cityscape across it. The world had been settled by both humans and Tralos, part of their loose alliance.

Veela: She stood at her captain's chair, watching the map on the screen. "Bring us in for landing."

Ray Athan: "Initiating landing procedures." He tapped his controls.

GM (Lizyin): The ship flew into the atmosphere, finding a landing pad at the spaceport without incident. Veela's archeological friend would be at the Daltive University, a professor there where he taught.

Veela: "Alright, everyone. Let's get packed and go visit by professor." She got herself ready, putting the orb in a backpack as she made her way out to find the university.

Ray Altan: He followed.

Dr. Donovan Conley: He came along with them.

Lt. Chandler: Chandler joined them.

Aria Benoit: The engineer brought up the rear.

Professor Scott (NPC): They made it to the university and found the office of Veela's friend Professor Scott, a long haired man with glasses and an eccentric look to him. He had just finished up his classes and seemed happy to see Veela. "Veela, my old student. What are you doing in this neck of the woods?"

Veela: Veela smiled at him. "Hello again. I hope we're not intruding."

Ray Altan: He looked at the various artifacts in the professor's office, curious, but careful not to touch.

Professor Scott (NPC): "I'm going to guess this is not a social call."

Veela: She grimaced. "Not exactly. I found a rare artifact and it appears the Aryshans are after it. I was wondering if you could tell me a little about it." She produced the orb and told him their adventures to try to find it int he first place.

Professor Scott (NPC): The professor listened with interest and then scrutinized the orb. "I see. I've heard of this planet before. There was an ancient civilization there, but we haven't had the funds to be able to explore it. It's said this race had quite the technology, things we might perceive as magic, and I believe this orb may be a remnant of that. We don't know what happened to them. We believe their fled their world and left the galaxy. But this orb is of immense power."

Ray Altan: He looked over. "We figured that much. But what does it do? Someone told us it could manipulate time?"

Professor Scott (NPC): "I don't know about that. I

believe these artifacts were said to interact telepathically with the wielder. It can create some kind of immense power, but beyond that, no one's ever had one of these before. I couldn't tell you."

Dr. Donovan Conley: "Well, the Aryshans seem to know something about it."

Professor Scott (NPC): "They're a secretive people. They have a history which is largely unknown to us. If I were you, I wouldn't want to tangle with them, though. Especially involving a telepathic device that could be used as a weapon. With their bondsense, they might be able to utilize the orb to a greater degree than we ever could."

Aria Benoit: She lingered toward the back of the group. "Still doesn't tell us what to do wit hit."

Professor Scott (NPC): He smiled. "That much is up to you."

Veela: "Would the Earth government be interested in such an artifact?"

Professor Scott (NPC): I would imagine thy would."

Lt. Chandler: "I would trust our people with it."

Ray Altan: He huffed. "Of course you would, ground pounder."

Lt. Chandler: He rolled his eyes at Ray.

Veela: "I don't think that's a bad idea. I trust Earth far more than I trust the alien on the station. Or the Aryshans for that matter."

Professor Scott (NPC): He watched and nodded.

Lt. Chandler: "I'll try to contact my people."

Veela: "Thank you for your help, Professor. We'll let you get back to work." Veela gave the professor a friendly nod at led her team out of there.

▭

#DM-Veela

Veela: Thanks I had fun last night. Thanks for taking me out.

Dr. Donovan Conley: No problem. Me too. You're a really special woman. Wish I could stay longer.

Veela: You heading out today?

Dr. Donovan Conley: Yeah, I'm in the airport now.

Veela: Well have a safe trip.

Dr. Donovan Conley: I'll try. Hopefully I'll be able to see you again.

Veela: I hope so too.

Dr. Donovan Conley: Plane's about to depart. See you on the flip side.

11

Jason

The Uber driver dropped Jason off at home. He was tired from too many nights out, along with too many full days of conferences. Maybe he was getting too old to party — even though he didn't go nearly as hard as his friends had.

All he'd been thinking about the whole way home was Rachel. He'd never felt a connection like this with anyone since… well, since he'd almost been married. It had been a couple of years since he'd let himself give into an attraction again, and he was not sure he wanted to get involved and risk wrecking another relationship.

Did he even have a relationship here? They'd had one meeting, one date, and their online experience. They lived halfway across the country from each other. What would come from it?

He'd always had a problem living in the moment, thinking things out, and extrapolating the future. It came from the analytics of his job, where he had to predict futures of different stocks and investment assets. The long term could matter just as much as the short term for his clients, and it worked much the same for life.

But why couldn't he enjoy it? Be happy with what he had with her. She liked him too; she'd said as much, so worrying about what might be or how their relationship would end would be pointless.

He shook his head as he carried his bags back into his house. It echoed as he entered, and it suddenly felt so empty. It was too big of a space for one person, never designed that way. But he couldn't just ask Rachel to move out here and in with him, could he? They only had known each other a short while.

"Just stop worrying," he told himself, setting his bags down and heading up the stairs. He'd unpack in the morning. Right now, he wanted to lay in his bed and get a good night's rest. He'd be back at it for work again tomorrow.

Once in his room, Jason flopped down onto his bed. It was nice to feel his mattress and sheets' firm yet soft cushioning. No matter how nice, a hotel room could never capture the feel of a home. Something about the way it smelled and felt was so comforting, even if the house was too big and empty for just him.

He was beat. His eyes didn't want to stay open, but Jason still had to get out of his clothes, change into something which didn't have all the germs of the flight on them, wash his face, and brush his teeth. Even though it wasn't much, he didn't have the energy or will to get up and do the routine.

Then, the doorbell rang.

Blood pumped through his veins, his heart beating hard as his fight or flight instinct kicked in. He sat up on the bed, a perplexed expression on his face. Who could have been here at this hour? He didn't have any appointments, and he hadn't set up any deliveries. Even though his fridge was undoubtedly empty save for expired items, he would wait until the following day to order food.

It could have been one of the neighbors. He tried to calm himself as he stood back up, ready to traverse back down the stairs. Adrenaline had him on high alert now.

He glanced toward his dresser drawer. Inside was a 9-millimeter Beretta, which he'd bought on a whim for protection. He'd only fired the thing a couple of times, but it was there for an emergency. He considered getting the gun out in case whoever stood at the front door meant to cause trouble, but would a criminal take the time to run the doorbell?

"Calm down," he told himself as he made his way back out of his room. He may have left some light on outside, or the neighbor might have needed a jump for their car. There had to be a simple explanation.

From the top of the stairs, he could see a figure standing at the door, though the glass to his entry had a frost, making it unable to see through. It came in handy when he lounged downstairs in his boxer shorts watching TV, able to run back up to his room and throw on some sweatpants quickly.

He wasn't in that situation, still with his pants and shoes on from the flight. He ran his hand back through his hair to ensure it was mostly in place before heading down the stairs.

The chime rang again.

"I'm coming," he said loud enough that it would likely be heard through the door. He finally reached the entryway and opened the door, more annoyed than frightened by this juncture.

A slender woman with dark hair, slightly curly, and the most innocent blue eyes stood on the porch, staring at him. She gave a bright smile and immediately brought Jason into an embrace. She kissed him on the cheek before standing back and giving him a once-over. "Jason, it's been so long!"

Her appearance startled him so much that he froze in place. He didn't react to the hug or the kiss. How could he? What was she even doing here? A lump formed in his throat, finding the situation so tense he could barely speak. "Danielle. What are you doing here?" He couldn't believe his ex stood before him.

"I've been spending some time thinking about life, everything that happened. I know it's a little late, but I figured I should talk to you in person rather than call or text. You always said it was better for important things." Her eyes darted to the side in a nervous tic she'd always had in difficult situations. But those eyes met his again with fierce intensity. "I want to try to work things out between us."

Space Adventures Online

#Daltive-IV

GM (Lizyin): On the way back to their ship, the streets of Daltive IV seemed seedier than one would find back on Earth. They didn't have the resources to police colony worlds like they did the ones back home, which left the place with its fair share of criminals and other underworld elements. Buildings rose on both sides of the street on the way to the spaceport, still a good ways off.

Veela: She walked down the street with her crew, the orb in her satchel which made it a little difficult to move quickly. "Well, I didn't expect to try to offload this to Earth, but I'll be grateful to get rid of it."

Ray Athan: "This mission brought us nothing but trouble. Didn't even get a payout."

Lt. Chandler: "The Earth government will pay fairly." He followed along.

Ray Athan: He rolled his eyes. "Fairly means we'll get nothing."

Dr. Donovan Conley: "I'm sure it won't be that bad." He stuck close by Veela.

Aria Benoit: She lingered along quietly.

GM (Lizyin): As they walked, four hooded figures approached the party and cut them off. No other witnesses seemed to be nearby. "Hand over the bag," one of them said to Veela.

Veela: She was taken aback, stepping backward as she couldn't really defend herself fin this position. "Leave us be. I'm warning."

Ray Athan: "Warning? Hell." He drew his pulse pistol.

Lt. Chandler: He didn't speak, but drew his weapon as well.

Dr. Donovan Conley: He didn't carry a weapon but balled his fists.

Aria Benoit: She pulled out a big monkey wrench.

GM (Lizyin): All of the hooded figures drew weapons, the one closest to Veela putting a knife to her throat while the others hand their pulse weapons.

Veela: She tried to escape the knife at her throat, backing up and swatting the arm away.

Ray Athan: He shot at the closest hooded figure, a quick draw as he prided himself in such.

Lt. Chandler: Chandler took the next one down the line, firing his gun.

Dr. Donovan Conley: Being close to Veela with no weapon to attack with, he kicked at the legs of the knife-wielding attacker.

Aria Benoit: Aria charged the fourth hooded person and swung her wrench at its head.

GM (Lizyin): Ray shot the hood right off the first one, which revealed an Aryshan! Chandler managed to down his target. Aria's stumbled but went into a grapple with her soon after— the Aryshan stronger than regular humans and managing to overtake her. Veela's had trouble fighting on two fronts, stumbling backward and dropping his knife.

Ray Athan: ((Is mine incapacitated?))

GM (Lizyin): ((Yes, sorry that wasn't clear.))

Veela: She tried to get out of the way of her attacker, to give her people a clear shot.

Ray Athan: He pointed his weapon directly at Veela's Aryshan and fired at its head.

Lt. Chandler: He ran for the one attacking Aria, dropping his weapon to try to pry his arms off of her.

Dr. Donovan Conley: He backed away trying to make sure he put himself between Veela and her assailant.

Aria Benoit: She kept trying to smash her wrench against the Aryshan on her. "Go. Down."

GM (Lizyin): Ray shot the one down in front of Veela and the attack seemed to go well against the fourth Aryshan. The grappled Aryshan stumbled from the hits but managed to draw a knife and dig it into Chandler's shoulder before he finally collapsed from getting hit from a wrench. They were out of combat for now.

Veela: She let out a deep breath. "Doctor. Help Chandler!"

Lt. Chandler: He ripped the knife out of his shoulder and grimaced.

Dr. Donovan Conley: He rushed over to Chandler to try to look at the wound. "Let me dress it."

Ray Athan: He kicked one of the Aryshans on the ground. "I'm sick of these Aryshans. All they seem to do is attack us."

Veela: "It's only been twice. But I am not interested in having them attack again. Let's get back to the ship and plan a meeting with an Earth representative immediately. I want this orb gone and out of our lives as fast as I can. Then… we'll try to figure out another job that actually pays." She nodded in firm resolve and then made her way back to their ship.

#DM-Dr.-Donovan-Conley

Veela: Hey Jason, I hope you made it home okay I'm sure you are probably asleep or whatnot at this point. I had a really good time while you were out here. See you in the game!

Rachel

Rachel wiped down the tables at the end of her next shift. After her whirlwind of the prior evening, she had to come back to reality sometime. To everyone else here, it might have been a simple night out, but spending time with Jason, allowing him to kiss her, she could hardly contain the buzz of excitement running through her veins. Even now, she could feel her every heartbeat.

She kept to herself while cleaning the tables, maneuvering chairs into place. Music played through the house speakers in the background, and the few patrons still present at the bar paid her no mind.

Jenny mopped the floor beside her, stopping and looking over at her with a casual smirk.

Rachel glanced up from her table after spraying disinfectant on it. "What?"

"You're humming."

"I am not."

"You are too. A stupid Journey song, too. I know you hate that kind of music." Jenny chuckled, shaking her head and pushing the mop across the floor.

Rachel tried to think a moment prior. Thoughts swirled in her mind about Jason. Sure enough, she found she had been humming a tune. What was wrong with her? She'd always been the quiet and reserved one among the staff at the bar.

Chris strolled by, an equally goofy look on his face as he'd heard the conversation. "It's because she had a date last night."

"Ohhhh yeah," Jenny said in a sing-song voice. Both she and Chris found too much amusement in this. It wasn't abnormal for someone to go out on a date. So why did they have to make fun of her?

"It wasn't a big deal," Rachel said, tossing her rag into a container with the dirty dishes. She was done with her cleaning chores for the evening and picked up the bin soon after.

"I haven't heard of you going on a date since you've worked here," Chris said with a shrug.

"It's because she hasn't gone on a date since she's worked here," Jenny added.

"You two are insufferable," Rachel huffed, delivering her tray to the kitchen window. "If you don't mind, I'm clocking out."

"Not going to give us any details?" Jenny asked.

Jenny sighed, turning toward her. "He's a nice guy, and I liked spending time with him. But he also lives in Reno, so it's not like I'm going to see him all the time. I don't even know if I'll see him again."

"Did you…" Jenny prodded suggestively.

"No!" Rachel crossed her arms. "Of course not. Who do you think I am?"

"I'm teasing." Jenny laughed again. "Well, I'm sure he was a gentleman if you let him take you out after your little coffee date."

"A second date?" Chris seemed to be half-listening as he reviewed the takes for the evening. "Now, this is serious."

"You two are the worst," Rachel said. "I don't know why I take this."

"Because you love us," Jenny said.

"Goodnight." Rachel promptly rushed toward the exit, not wanting to deal with any more grilling for the evening. She'd already had enough of their brand of teasing, and she didn't much like it. Even though it was harmless, Rachel couldn't help but feel like she was under a microscope. It added to her already bad anxiety over life. It was why she wasn't social to begin with.

Jenny knew this, which annoyed her, but she would get over it. They meant to be friendly, and Rachel couldn't hold it against them. She could only head out into the cooling Nashville night air to her car, wishing Jason lived closer to her.

Maybe she would look for a job in Reno. What was keeping her here anyway? Sure, she'd spent time here for the last four-plus years, but college had ended a long time ago, and she had been trying to apply for real jobs until she'd all but given up on the prospect.

What could there be with international relations in a small city in Nevada, though? She'd have to look for something different. She couldn't be a cocktail waitress forever.

But then, Jason was independently wealthy. Maybe....

No, She couldn't allow herself into that line of thought. She'd taken care of herself thus far and wasn't about to rely on someone else to take care of her. Not until children were in the discussion, at least.

The thought caused Rachel to freeze outside of her car. Had she thought about having children with this man she'd only been out with twice? Rachel shook her head to clear her mind. She'd never even considered the prospect before now. There had never been a man who'd seemed stable enough to raise a family.

She had to admit she had it bad for Jason. Why else would she be thinking about this? But she still had to take it one day at a time. He liked her, obviously from how he kissed her the night prior, but who knew what was going through his mind now?

At least the game would keep her mind occupied for a while, even if she'd struck up a romance with his character there too. In the game, at least, she had something else to soother than fixate on a man.

Space Adventures Online

#Sunflower

▭

Veela: She entered the bridge of the starship, flustered from the day's events with Aryshans attacking them on a human colony. How had they gotten there? Did they have to worry they were being followed by a bigger ship? She couldn't worry too much about it, as she would be rendezvousing with the Earth frigate *Warsaw* in a few hours. "Status report," she said, sounding as official as she could.

Ray Athan: He sat at the piloting console. "FTL drive holding strong. E.T.A. two and a half hours."

Lt. Chandler: He stood at tactical, ready in case the Aryshans did follow them and attack.

Veela: "Thank you, Mr. Athan. Hopefully our friends are on time."

Lt Chandler: "And our enemies don't realize where we're going." He wasn't so hopeful.

Veela: She couldn't wait to get out of this, pacing the bridge in nervousness. All they had to do was offload this orb and they could get back to business as usual. Perhaps a nice simple cargo run from one port to another, even though it wouldn't be something terribly profitable, it would make for a nice change of pace.

GM (Lizyin): The ship rattled in a strange way, something feeling off.

Veela: She hit her comm. "Aria, what's goin on down there?"

Aria Benoit: "Engines seem to be normal. I don't know."

Veela: "Well, figure it out. I don't want to be torn apart in FTL."

Aria Benoit: "Working on it."

GM (Lizyin): the source of the rattling seems to come from the orb, which brought out this giant waft of energy, a bright light which seemed to consume everything on the bridge.

Ray Athan: He shielded his eyes. "What in the name of…"

Lt. Chandler: "This orb is dangerous." He tried to move toward it to see if there was some way he could turn the energy off.

Veela: She could feel the energy, and knew there was something drastically wrong. She scrambled toward the orb as well.

GM (Lizyin): It was like there was a forcefield around it, stopping them. They couldn't get close to the orb.

Veela: "We can't get near it. Options?"

GM (Lizyin): Just then, the ship fell out of FTL into the middle of space. They were nowhere near their rendezvous.

Ray Athan: "We're out of FTL. I can't get us going." Ray tapped frantically at his console.

Aria Benoit: "I'm sorry, captain. I have no idea what's going on. I wish I could help!"

Veela: "It's not your fault, Aria. It's this orb."

Lt. Chandler: He tried to look for any holes or anything in the forcefield, any way he could get toward the orb.

GM (Lizyin): He would find none. The Orb just kept producing more and more energy. Even engineering filled with light now. It was activated somehow, and it kept pulsing, growing stronger. Worse for the Sunflower, if Ray looked at his scanners, two Aryshan warships would be appearing just off their bow, flanking the ship.

———————————————————————

12

Jason

———————————————————————

Jason decided to table discussions until the morning. He offered Danielle one of his guest rooms for her to stay the night before they got into the serious topics of their relationship. He was too tired to think, and it wasn't a good time, but he didn't want to turn her away.

Danielle had come from where she'd been staying in San Francisco, her life in the finance industry, working downtown in the business district south of Market. It took about a four-hour drive to get to Reno, and she should have called him before coming, which she agreed when he pointed it out, but her spontaneity had gotten the best of her, and she made it here.

They'd met initially on an internship working for some analytics for a bank. It was a fun time in the office, with about half the time spent competing on mobile games and hiding phones and browsers when the manager came by to watch them work. Their messing around only led to long work days where they spent too much time together. Jason and Danielle couldn't help but get close.

It led to happy hour dates at different bars in the financial district, by the ferry building, and more formal dates. Everything progressed naturally and smoothly until their jobs took them in different directions.

They both made good money in finance, but Danielle's work took her across the country. It had always felt distant from that point forward. She'd travel so much; he'd be alone watching TV. Even though they'd come close to getting married to sharing this new house when they both progressed to a point where they could work remotely, their connection seemed to have faded by that point.

She put too much of herself into her career, and Jason wanted someone he could be close with and feel like she was his partner. Unfortunately, it was lonely, and with the prospect of moving to Reno and away from everyone they knew, it would only get lonelier.

He'd gone out to a bar one evening with friends, had too much to drink, and went home with a girl he had a great conversation with. He didn't excuse himself for his moment of weakness, it still ate him inside that he'd gotten to that point, but their relationship had gone sour by then, and neither of them could admit it.

As Danielle sat at his kitchen counter while he made her eggs and sausage for breakfast, wearing short sweat shorts and a t-shirt with her hair in a ponytail, she seemed unready to admit it.

The worst part was, after an evening of barely being able to sleep because the thought of their past kept him up, Jason couldn't be sure what he wanted either.

"Breakfast's ready," he said, sliding the eggs from the non-stick pan to the plate with expert precision. A few years back, he'd learned how to make eggs over-medium and not break the yolks, something he remained proud of to this day.

Danielle gazed up at him with a warm smile. "Thank you."

"Don't worry about it." Jason fixed his plate and sat beside her at the counter. He picked at his food with his fork, unsure what to say.

"I'm sorry I laid that on you last night. I'd meant to talk first, get us back knowing each other again. It's been months, and I'm sure we've both grown as people. I… I just wanted to let you know I forgive you. I should have been there more for you; I was dismissive; I can empathize with why you, you know." Her eyes bored into him, not abashed at all by what she was saying.

It made Jason severely uncomfortable. He had to look down at his food. "No, there's no excusing what I did. I should have talked. We might have worked things out. I needed to learn how to communicate that there's a problem."

"Well, we're communicating now."

He looked up at her again. She had the cutest of smiles. Why did she have to pop back into his life now of all times? He'd just met Rachel, and Rachel was a fresh start for him, someone he felt he could communicate with, someone he wanted to be online talking to now more than anything. And yet, this was a relationship that had gone years. Should he abandon it for a girl he'd only met a couple of times on the internet?

The thought of all of it gave him a headache. He cut his egg, watching the yolk bleed out onto the plate before he scooped some up and took a bite. At least breakfast could give him an excellent excuse to appear occupied and not as chatty as Danielle wanted to be. All of this just felt wrong.

And yet he couldn't bear to tell her to leave.

"How long are you in town for?" He asked.

"I hadn't decided," Danielle said. "I took a week off work. I have three months of vacation accrued. I never take any, as you know."

"I remember." They'd never gone anywhere together. Jason took time off to have days away from the office, but their travel was limited to their work functions, usually separate.

"So I can stay awhile. Maybe get to know you again."

If he tried to make this work, he would have to give her time to see if they could talk and coexist. Was this what he wanted? He glanced at the microwave clock and nearly jumped out of his chair.

"Crap. I'm late for a conference call. I gotta get on the phone. Uh, make yourself at home. Okay?"

Before she could respond, he had already booked it out of the kitchen and toward his office. Solving the problems of his relationships would have to wait because he still had his work to do.

Space Adventures Online

#General

—

Veela: Has anyone seen Conley online?

Ray Athan: Not since he was out in your neck of the woods.

Veela: Hmm. We can't really get the scene going again without him. Too much could happen here to lose one of the crew.

Lizyin: Maybe he's just busy with work?

Veela: Could be.

Ray Athan: Or maybe he's running for the hills.

Aria Benoit: You're a jerk, Ray.

Ray Athan: I know.

Veela: I hope that's not the case.

Ray Athan: Wouldn't be very fun to be out a doctor, especially as we're getting into some more danger.

Aria Benoit: She's also going to lose her character's

relationship if he doesn't come back. You could be a little more sensitive.

Ray Athan: Me?

Veela: It's okay. I don't want to think about it. Let's change the subject.

Aria Benoit: Well, my house flooded in the storm last week. Looks like I'm going to have a lot of damage and the insurance company is giving me a runaround.

Ray Athan: Oof.

Veela: Sorry to hear that Aria.

Lizyin: Sorry.

Aria Benoit: I don't know where I'm gonna find the money to fix this. But I can't really do anything about it.

Veela: Hopefully insurance comes through.

Veela: Yeah.

#DM-Ray-Athan

Ray Athan: What happened with you and Conley?

Veela: I'm not sure I should talk about it. I don't know if he wants me to.

Ray Athan: But you met up.

Veela: Yeah.

Ray Athan: And…?

Veela: Not what you're thinking. He was a gentleman.

Ray Athan: Hmm.

Veela: What?

Ray Athan: Sounds like he didn't like you that much in person. Sorry to be frank, but just being honest.

Veela: :(

Ray Athan: Maybe it's not a big deal. Who knows?
Veela: I guess we'll find out soon.
Ray Athan: Here's to hoping the best.

———

#DM-Dr.-Donovan-Conley

———

Veela: Hey Jason, I haven't seen you on in a couple of days and hope there's not something wrong. I had a really good time with you and really enjoy talking to you. Anyway, I hope everything's okay. Don't be a stranger.

Two full days passed, and Rachel hadn't heard from Jason since the flight. She checked her phone every few minutes, hoping he might have sent a direct message. But it remained blank. Even her other friends on the chat weren't messaging her, not that that was abnormal; she spent more time in D.M. with Jason than she had with the others.

There had been days going by where they hadn't talked. At least, a few weeks ago. Since then, it had been a steady progression of them chatting or playing until his trip out to Nashville.

Now, nothing.

It couldn't help but stick in Rachel's head. Had she been too cold to him? Had she come on too strong? She couldn't figure out what the problem might have been. He'd seemed interested enough when he was out here with her. He was the one who pushed for a second meeting.

Did he want to kiss her and then get cold feet? God, this sent her for a loop. She hadn't questioned herself or whether someone liked her since high school. There had been a couple of boys she'd had crushes on who hurt her back then, leaving her crying in her room. It seemed her whole life she'd never really been able to find someone to connect with on a level where she felt comfortable, and when she felt uncomfortable, she could come across as standoffish.

Replaying their meetings in her mind, Rachel couldn't think of a time when she'd come across as uninterested in him. It had to have been coming on too strong. But he'd made every move, even the kiss. It was all so confusing.

Rachel pressed her fingers to her lips, remembering the feel of the kiss, his warm lips against hers, firm, holding her in his arms. All she wanted to do was to go back to that night and make it last for an eternity. Why did he have to live across the country?

That could be it. He could have been uncomfortable with the long distance and wanted to cut it off before their relationship went too far.

Or she could have been overthinking things. She fell back onto her mattress, bouncing on it from the force of her descent. Her head rested on her pillow, looking at the white ceiling. The spots of texture seemed to move ever so slightly as she stared at it. She'd always wondered why that was the case.

Before she could get too comfortable, her phone rang.

Rachel scrambled to her nightstand to swipe at her phone and grab it. She looked at the screen. Her father called her.

Groaning, Rachel answered the phone. "Hello?"

"Rachel, darling. How are you? We hadn't heard from you in almost a week."

Because she didn't feel much like talking to her parents. "I've just been working a lot."

"I see," her father said. He paused ominously, sounding like he was judging her as he always did. "Your mother met a nice man down at church on Sunday. Single. Has a nice job. I think you should come and meet him."

"I don't have time to come out there. I've got work."

"Are you still waitressing?"

"Yes."

Another long pause. Her father let out a deep sigh. "That's not exactly a real job, is it? They'll understand if you take off for a few days."

She didn't want to meet whoever her mom was trying to set her up with. Especially not now. She had Jason. Didn't she? As she thought of her situation again, she sucked in her bottom lip. Maybe she was being too foolish waiting on this guy all the way from Nevada. What if he didn't want her at all?

"Rachel?" Her dad asked.

"Sorry. I don't know. It's hitting the end of the tourist season. Maybe next month?"

He projected his annoyance in the way he breathed. "Rachel, after a long talk with your mother, we're willing to cover your student debt next year if you come home. You don't have to waste your life waitressing. We get how hard it can be to find a job. What do you think?"

"Wow…" Rachel was flabbergasted. They'd offered her a place to stay to come home but never really to take her debt away. Her parents must have really wanted her back. As she thought about it, she didn't love her waitressing job. Nor did she like her life here after college. All of her friends had gone away. She barely had any social life. It wouldn't be that different in South Carolina than here, would it?

"You can think about it. Take your time. But why don't you come home and scope things out like I'm saying, see if it feels right?"

It was as if her father knew what to say this time. It

wasn't like the last time they talked when he'd been so cold to her. Guilt swelled within Rachel. She'd been so neglectful of her family. Why? To be stubborn, she could make it on her own? It seemed so foolish now.

He'd trapped her. Just like he'd intended, but she couldn't refuse him either. "Okay. I'll talk to my boss and see if I can get a couple of days off and come home for the weekend."

"Wonderful, honey. We'll see you then. You can stay for as long as you'd like." She could almost hear him smiling through the phone.

She hung up, laying back on her bed again. Everything in her life felt like a whirlwind—or going nowhere. Why couldn't Jason just come online and let her know what was going on? At least then, she wouldn't have to think about it anymore.

Space Adventures Online

#General

Lizyin (GM): Alright. I think enough time's gone by. We should just assume Conley is an NPC and get the game going again. Everyone good with that?
Ray Athan: Of course.
Aria Benoit: Yeah, I wanna play.
Lt. Chandler: Sure.
Veela: … I don't like leaving him but I guess so.
Lizyin (GM): To #Sunflower then.

#Sunflower

Lizyin (GM): The two Aryshan ships appeared to be coming closer. They powered up their weapons.

Lt. Chandler: "The Aryshans have powered up their weapons!"

Veela: "Shields!" She gripped the sides of her chair. Not like the shields would do much in a situation like this.

Ray Athan: He did his best at the piloting console to try to keep them a moving target.

Lizyin (GM): A communications signal came in.

Veela: "Put the signal on audio."

Lt. Chandler: He raised shields and opened the audio channel.

Nirral (NPC): "Greetings human vessel. I am Commander Nirral of the Aryshan Warship *Stelvyr*. Prepare to surrender your orb and be boarded."

Veela: "We'll never let you get the orb."

Nirral (NPC): "Then you will die."

Veela: "If you shoot us up, you'll lose the orb."

Lizyin (GM): The Aryshan ship shot a grappling hook at the Sunflower and caught them in its grip. It pulled the Sunflower toward the warship.

Ray Athan: He frowned, seeing what was going on. "Looks like they called our bluff."

Veela: "There has to be some way out of it. Can we shoot the hook off?"

Lt. Chandler: He tried to target the grappling hook's cable and fire at it.

Lizyin (GM): The cable proved too small to target reliably and the pulse weapons seemed to have no effect.

Lt. Chandler: "No effect, captain."

Veela: "Dammit." She bit her lip. What could she do? She looked back at the orb, floating there, bright. "Curse you, do something!"

Lizyin (GM): As if on command, the orb brightened

again, blinding the bridge of the Sunflower and everyone nearby. The ship rocked as energy came shooting from it. Engineering had an explosion in the plasma pipelines.

Lt. Chandler: He stumbled at his station but caught the railing.

Ray Athan: He tried to steady the ship with the console, though he couldn't see so he did his best to work his magic.

Aria Benoit: "I've got an explosion down here! Working to contain it!" She programmed her bots to do the work so she wouldn't get caught in anything harmful.

Veela: She shielded her eyes, unsure what was going on.

Lizyin (GM): When they could see again, Ray would find they had no star charts around them, no recognizable landscape, simply a bright, brilliant light all around them. White space instead of the blackness of normal space. They seemed to have disappeared from their reality entirely.

Ray Athan: "I think we entered some kind of other dimension. I have no idea what's going on. Instruments aren't responding."

Lt. Chandler: He shook his head. "The Aryshan ships seem to be nowhere nearby."

Veela: "Engineering? Is everything okay?"

Aria Benoit: "The plasma leak seems to be contained for now."

Veela: She stared at the screen in front of her, the whiteness everywhere. Where were they and what could they possibly be doing here? "Scan the outside. See if there's anything there."

Lt. Chandler: He ran his scans.

Lizyin (GM): Chandler would find nothing but breathable air.

Lt. Chandler: "It seems like there's an atmosphere out there. Temperature is comfortable for humans. It's almost as if we're being invited outside."

Veela: She frowned, shaking her head. "It seems whatever this orb thing is, it wants us to explore, or perhaps bring it home. Let's open the back hatch and see what we can find."

13

Jason

The last two days had gone better than Jason expected. Old habits died hard, and he found himself comfortable with Danielle. They'd spent so much time together before they'd drifted apart that it was only natural to enjoy her company again.

They did a lot together, considering she'd just arrived. Danielle helped him with shopping to refill his empty fridge. Jason was never very good at finding small items like bean paste or the different kinds of tomato sauces in a supermarket. There were too many options, too many aisles. Danielle navigated his shopping list like a pilot taking a plane in for a landing. She also managed to pick up a few items he hadn't thought of for snacks and drinks. It was nice having a woman around in the house.

The evenings also had a nice pleasantness to them, where Danielle worked on cooking for him—something he rarely did himself. Cooking for one was difficult, not generally worth the effort. He typically ordered out, even though that wasn't exactly the healthiest of options. It made for a simpler evening and clean-up. Still, he liked having home-cooked meals—with the bonus of having leftovers for lunch the next day.

They spent a lot of time together talking, catching up on the last year or so, and watching different television shows or movies. The routine came naturally, much like their relationship had before. Maybe it was for the best?

One evening, Jason saw his Space Adventures Online tab. He hadn't logged in since Danielle arrived, far too occupied and not having any alone time to play the game. It had been such a fun couple of months, but now that he'd fallen out of the habit of playing, did he need to go back on there?

He bit his lower lip, recalling Rachel. Talking to her had been such a different experience in life. They'd clicked in a way he'd never felt with anyone before, Danielle included. But she also lived halfway across the country. Could he gamble on a future there when he had someone stable here? He didn't know what to do but couldn't log in now. There'd be too many questions, and he wouldn't want to be coy with the answers. He owed Rachel the truth if anything, but he couldn't give her the truth when he hadn't decided.

"Jaaaason," Danielle said in a sing-song voice. "It's time to watch Witches of Fairyland."

Danielle's show. It was on a girlie network where they presented fantasy concepts as low-key romance stories. Jason never liked the show, but he'd tolerated it and watched it with Danielle for several seasons because it was something to do to spend time with her. They'd had so little time when they were both grinding out their jobs. Any togetherness was a bonus.

Now, he didn't want to deal with it. He wondered if life would settle back into this, with Danielle pursuing her career, leaving him alone again, making the same mistakes again. And her friends. He'd forgotten how obnoxious they were. Catty women whose entire existence seemed to be trying to one-up each other with the latest fashions or life statuses. As much as he enjoyed having a comfortable lifestyle, Jason didn't do it for the show. He didn't want people looking at him, scrutinizing whether he was worthy based on his material possessions.

Rachel would never do that. She was down to earth. God, what should he do?

"I'm coming," he finally answered dutifully. For now, he had to live here, in real life, in the moment, and enjoy his time with Danielle. Eventually, though, he'd have to make a real decision.

He pushed his chair back from his desk and returned to the living room, where Danielle sat on the couch, wearing one of his hoodies. It draped over her as if she were a giant, but she used it more as a blanket than an actual garment. She smiled up at him. "Everything okay?"

"Yeah." Jason flopped down on the couch. There wasn't anything that mattered, but something didn't feel right about this whole situation. He couldn't quite put a finger on it.

Danielle cocked her head at him curiously. "There's a problem."

"There's not."

"There is. I've seen this look before."

They both stared at each other for a long moment. Jason used his lips, trying to figure out what to say. He had a hard time articulating how he felt. Why was this so difficult? Because it was wrong. Because he'd fostered a relationship elsewhere, and this seemed like he was cheating on Rachel.

It was absurd. They had no relationship beyond the one their characters had online. They had a minor encounter in person, but they hadn't discussed plans or made any commitments. Why couldn't he live in the moment and figure things out later?

Because he knew Danielle had come here for more than a fling. She wanted to rekindle their relationship from before. The one where they had almost built a permanent life together. He couldn't do that here and now.

She didn't push the matter, though. Instead, Danielle leaned her head against him on the couch, grabbed the remote, and pointed it at the TV. She flipped the app to her streaming service and pulled up the display for Witches of Fairyland. Jason tensed, unable to relax with her touching him. More, he didn't want to watch this show. He wished he could get back online, but there was no way he could sneak out and do that. Not without too many questions he didn't want to answer.

Resigned, Jason slumped into the couch and turned his attention to the show. At least while the TV was on, they wouldn't have to talk about anything serious.

Space Adventures Online

#General

⸻

Veela: Hey everyone, what's up?

Aria Benoit: Not much. Heard from Conley?

Veela: No. :(

Aria Benoit: I'm sorry.

Ray Athan: Just another fader, it looks like.

Veela :Huh?

Ray Athan: A lot of people come online for role-play because they can't get that high in real life. They get a little boost from 'the chase' romances. Once the chase is gone, they 'fade to black'. Hence, fader.

Veela: Well that's a cynical way of looking anti t.

Ray Athan: Honey, I've been playing on these games for ten plus years, I've seen everything.

Aria Benoit: You're still a jerk. This isn't what Veela needs to hear.

Ray Athan: It's the truth.

Aria Benoit: It doesn't matter. There's tactful ways to say things, and then there's you.

Ray Athan: Whatever. Buzz off.

Lizyin (GM): Stop fighting, people or I'm going to time both of you out.

Veela: It's fine. Maybe Ray's right. I don't know. It's weird to have someone on here so hot and then disappear so fast.

Ray Athan: He got what he wanted.

Aria Benoit: I swear to god…

Lt. Chandler: Ray, it's time to shut up.

Ray Athan: Don't white knight for Aria.

Lt. Chandler: I'm not.

Aria Benoit: I've put up with your stuff long enough, Ray. Leave Veela alone. I know how she feels. She thought someone really liked her and he's gone. It hurts.

Ray Athan: Well that's why you don't put your faith in random people on the internet. You never know where they're really coming from.

Veela: …I think I'm gonna log off now.

Lizyin (GM): You don't want to play? I have the scene all ready.

Veela: No. I can't get in the mood for role-play. Not now.

Aria Benoit: See what you did, Ray?

Ray Athan: This isn't my fault, it's Conley's.

Lt. Chandler: Seriously, Ray.

Ray Athan: Seriously yourself. You all suck.

[Ray Athan has been placed on a 10 minute time out from the moderator]

Aria Benoit: Thank you.

Lizyin (GM): Emotions are running high right now. You're not helping either, Aria. Let's just all settle down and we'll run a scene later when Veela feels like it. Okay?

Aria Benoit: Okay.

Lt. Chandler: I'll be here.

Veela: Thanks for understanding, guys.

Aria Benoit: No problem. I know how you feel. Hope everything works out.

#DM-Lizyin

Lizyin: Hey, I hope Ray didn't bother you too much.

Veela: No, he's totally right about this. I shouldn't get so invested in an online relationship. It's okay. I'm going home to my parents house this weekend. I'll reset my life and my priorities, get everything back on track.

Lizyin: Good. If you need anything, I'm here for you, okay?

Veela: Thanks, Lizyin. The game's been so great the last few months. I appreciate you.

Lizyin: I like running plots for you.

Veela: See you around.

Lizyin: Later.

Rachel

Rachel pulled into the driveway of her parents' South Carolina suburban home. The track housing development was built at least twenty years ago. It was new when Rachel arrived, but it looked dated now. Still, she preferred it to the modern houses. The new ones all tended to look cookie-cutter, the same.

Her parents' house, by contrast, had a nice brick exterior with a couple of white columns out front. It wasn't large or extravagant by any means, but it was still the old style where they had a lot with no fence, open to greenery, nice and spacious along a suburban road. Many of the houses back in Nashville had a similar style; it was all southern and home.

She stepped out of the car, memories flooding back into her of when she lived here. Her mom took her to soccer games as a child, rushing her out the door. Sneaking out to parties in high school, hoping her dad didn't catch her running down the street while her friends waited a block away with their lights off. It was comforting, warm, and home. It was much different than her apartment, where it seemed like a place to sleep.

Her parents saw her approaching and opened the door before she could knock on it. Her mom stood there, eyes beaming with pride, a smile across her face. She looked slightly older than Rachel remembered her, a little more gaunt in the face. Not unhealthy, but the age and wear on her started her. It seemed like yesterday her mother was in her thirties, making dinner in the kitchen for her.

Whatever her mother's appearance, she was still her mother. Rachel hugged her and squeezed tightly, happy to see her. "Hi, mom."

"Honey. You're looking good." Of course, her mother would have said that no matter how Rachel looked.

"Thanks." Rachel pulled back and looked up at her dad, then embraced him similarly. "Dad."

"Good to see you, darling. Do you have bags?" Her father asked.

"Just one. I packed pretty light."

"Let me get it for you."

"I can."

Her father stepped past her toward the car. He was ever the gentleman and wouldn't let a lady carry her heavy bag if he didn't have to. It was an endearing quality.

"Come on in," her mother said, ushering her inside.

The place looked much the same as it had before. Family pictures adorned the entry walls and the hallway to the kitchen and living room beyond. Her parents had an old sofa with a flower print—dated but still nice looking. One feature that had changed was the fireplace in the room was of the gas variety, with a glass face to it, flame flickering in the background.

"When'd you change the fireplace?" Rachel asked as she made her way into the room.

"A few months ago. Our neighbors got one, and you turn it on by pushing a button on a remote. Seems better than burning wood," her mother said.

"Much easier, at least. It doesn't have the same smell, though."

"That's probably a good thing."

"True."

Her father entered backed into the room with her bag in tow, setting it down on the floor beside the couch. "Are you hungry, Rachel?" he asked.

"No, I ate some fast food on the way."

"You shouldn't have," her mother said. "It's bad for you, and I would have made you a nice home-cooked meal."

Rachel shrugged. "I didn't think about it. Sorry."

"Well, why don't you get settled in your room and come join us for dinner anyway? A lot to talk about." Her father smiled at her.

He didn't hide his plans to talk about her moving back in, and he wanted to make her comfortable with the memory of her old home. Rachel could already see it coming. She didn't want her parents pressuring her, but having some alone time in her room would give her a bit to think about how to respond.

And then there was this guy they wanted to set her up with. She wasn't sure she was ready for that discussion either.

"Okay," Rachel said, picking up her bag. She headed back down the hall to the line of rooms comprising her bedroom, her father's office, and a guest room. The master bedroom was on the opposite wing.

When she entered her room, it felt so old and distant. Her pink bedding didn't match her current lifestyle, nor did the white desk with a lot of her high school pictures pinned to it. Her wall still had a poster of a TV show that had gone off the air three years ago, her favorite at the time. It was a romance, and it was kind of dumb in hindsight. Since she'd gotten into these books and role-playing, her tastes had changed dramatically.

It had made her nerdier. She couldn't help but chuckle to herself as she thought about it.

Regardless, it wasn't bad to be back home. She flopped back onto her bed, letting the mattress bounce. It was a little softer than her current bed in her apartment, almost uncomfortably so. Probably because she'd gotten used to the new one. It was strange how tastes changed based on what one was used to.

And immediately, she found herself reaching for her laptop in her bag. She got it out of the front pouch and opened it up. Old habits died hard. Her parents would be waiting for her, but she had a little time before they called her to dinner. She could check in on the game, see how her crew was doing, and see if she could get a scene going.

Though, in truth, she wanted to see if Jason logged on and messaged her. As she logged into the game, she prayed he would be there.

#General

Veela: Hey everybody.

Lt. Chandler: Hey, Veela.

Lizyin (GM): Veela! How's the 'rents house?

Veela: A little awkward so far. You know what they say, 'you can't go home again.'

Ray Athan: Except you just did. Literally.

Lt. Chandler: Are you always a contrarian, Ray?

Ray Athan: Just stating the obvious.

Veela: lol. No it's okay. I did do just that. It's just weird. Seems like the ghost of an old home, if that makes any sense.

Lt. Chandler: It does. I didn't go back home to my parents until ten years after I moved out. It was an odd experience. Everything seemed dated and dusty. I know I don't talk about my out of character life much, but I can tell you're in a mood and want you to know you have friends here.

Veela: I appreciate it, and I know what you mean. Though not a lot of dust here. My mom likes things really clean.

Lt. Chandler: So did mine, other than the dust. I swear she just let things sit for years. The house smells strange now.

Veela: I only smell chicken cooking.

Ray Athan: Send me some. I'm hungry.

Veela: Would if I could. I ate before I got here. Still no sign of Conley?

Lizyin (GM): No, unfortunately.

Veela: Figured not.

Ray Athan: If he did show up, I'm sure he'd DM you first before talking to any of us.

Veela: Probably true. Oh well. Hey, I'll be back on later tonight after dinner and talking to my parents. We can maybe boot up our plot then?

Lizyin (GM): I'll be there.

Lt. Chandler: Sounds good.

Ray Athan: Yep.

#Sunflower

Veela: Veela stepped from the ramp of the ship into the white space. She took in a breath just to make sure there was air.

Lizyin (GM): There was air.

Veela: ((Lol, nice description.))

Lizyin (GM): ((I aim to please.))

Lt. Chandler: The security officer followed, weapon at the ready, and ever vigilant in scanning the area.

Ray Athan: He stretched his arms out, happy to be on the move and not sitting at a helm console.

Aria Benoit: She took readings of this place with her scanner, trying to get a clue as to the space's composition.

Lizyin (GM): Her readings would show haywire scans that were gibberish. The atmosphere seemed stable but she couldn't glean anything about the area. It seemed to go on for infinity.

Veela: "Well, this is where the orb wanted us. Do you see anything we should be doing?" She glanced around.

Lt. Chandler: "Nothing I can see so far."

Aria Benoit: "My scanner isn't giving me anything useful." She whapped it on the side just in case it would make it work.

Lizyin (GM): It chirped at her in protest when she accidentally hit a button, but didn't give her any more information.

Ray Athan: "Sure beats being killed by Aryshans." He chuckled.

Veela: "True enough. But I still want to figure out what's going on and get us back home again." She stepped further into the white space.

Lizyin (GM): Out of the mist formed a nine foot being. Long legs, long arms, beady eyes and four of them. The being was grey, ribs protruding through its skin. It had a small mouth compared to its being.

Lt. Chandler: He drew his pulse pistol, not sure what he was looking at but not going to risk his captain getting hurt.

Aria Benoit: "I think this creature might know the

answers to whatever you're asking." She pointed to the alien.

Ray Athan: He tried to look cool and collected but was ready to dart back to the ship on a moment's notice.

Veela: She wasn't scared. She stepped up to the alien to try to uncover the mystery. This had to be one of the ancient Kraleen who had inhabited Aetheon where they had found the orb. "Hello. My name is Captain Veela of the cargo freighter, Sunflower. We were brought here by a mysterious orb. What is it, and who are you?"

Rr'rink (NPC): The alien creature watched them with curiosity, something inside it translating their language. "Greetings. My name is Rr'rink. I am of the Kraleen and I see you have found our Orb of Reckoning. We evolved from our home planet, expanding outward upon thousands of generations. Finally, we ascended outside of your galaxy, leaving behind many of our artifacts on our journey outward into the unknown. You currently occupy a space outside of what you consider your reality, outside of your time. It Is impossible to describe to you in a way your minds would comprehends. However, with your ingenuity, you have made it this far. It is an achievement."

Veela: She glanced back at the others.

Ray Athan: He just shrugged. "Thanks, I think."

Aria Benoit: "We were being chased and almost killed for this orb. Can you help us?"

Rr'rink (NPC): "I have an oath to keep my distance from lower life forms. Therefore, I cannot help nor interfere. I will, however, take the technology from you. It is not meant for the lower races to possess." With that proclamation, he raised his hand and extracted the orb from the ship. It appeared in his hand, out of thin air. "Thank you for bringing it here."

Veela: "Well that's a load of bull. We went through hell

to get this thing. And we get nothing for it?" She narrowed her eyes.

Rr'rink (NPC): The creature looked at her. "Material matters are irrelevant. You will find this when you complete your corporeal existence. Enjoy the experience." With that, the alien creature disappeared.

Lt. Chandler: He tried to fire his pulse pistol at the creature. It stole form them after all.

Lizyin (GM): The pulse fizzled in the whiteness, completely ineffective.

Lt. Chandler: He cursed under his breath.

Veela: "Easy come easy go, but how do we get out of here?'

Rr'rink (NPC): "Your ship will be transported by us. Leave now." A disembodied voice said.

Ray Athan: He backpedaled toward the ship. As much has he'd had fun earlier, these creatures creeped him out. "I ain't gonna get caught here stuck."

Aria Benoit: She turned around and followed Ray, staying close to him. "Me either."

Veela: She stood there for a long time in disbelief. That was it? They got nothing for their troubles. It was unbelievable. She turned, heading back to her ship, angry, stomping the whole way.

Lt. Chandler: He followed, still keeping an eye out to protect his captain in case any threats followed.

Lizyin (GM): They made it back into the ship without incident, no longer to see anything but the whiteness. The orb and Rr'rink were gone.

14

Jason

The fifth day Danielle had been staying with him, Jason started to remember why they'd had troubles. She started critiquing his routine, early work morning, his break for working out around ten o'clock, and late lunches. Even though he thought he kept his house pretty clean, she complained about it and the way Jason had organized the furniture.

"I don't think I'm going to change it right now," Jason said, looking at his phone and wanting to escape. The problem was, she was here; he couldn't get away.

"You're not listening to me," Danielle said, crossing her arms.

"I am. Would the couch be better if it were angled at forty-five degrees? I don't care and don't want to move it."

"That's your problem, you know? You never care about the details. This is exactly what frustrated me so much back in the day. It's the same with our relationship." Danielle shook her head.

Jason stood there a little stunned. They were starting a fight over nothing. They'd done this so many times before.

The memories came flooding back to him—bickering over food, screaming over who broke their cabinets, passive-aggressive silent treatment over some words they exchanged in which Jason didn't even remember what they'd said to this day.

Beyond having schedules and travel, which made it so they didn't see each other enough, this was why he'd started to feel distant from Danielle. They didn't mesh together. His heart felt like a heavy weight had been draped around it, dragging it downward.

Getting back together had been her idea. She'd wanted to try to make it work, and Jason always knew it didn't feel quite right the entire time, but now he had a much more concrete reason why. He liked not being alone. It was nice to have someone there to share moments with, even if it weren't ideal, but Danielle and he just weren't compatible.

"There's something wrong," Danielle said, her eyes seeming to pierce into him. "I see it on your face. You have that pensive look."

"I do not."

"You do too."

"I do not."

Her brow furrowed. "Seriously, Jason? What are we, twelve?"

"I don't think I'm being immature here. You're the one who's in my house and telling me I need to rearrange my furniture." He walked over to the wall and leaned against it. He was unsure why he moved there but wanted to be a little further apart from her.

She paced across the room, behind the couch, and flopped down on it. She glanced downward, clearly upset with the whole situation. "I thought I could come here and make this work. I miss you, Jason."

"I miss you too."

"It's nice hanging out with you."

"It is." And hanging out is what it was. Despite coming close to cuddling while watching television, nothing was physical about their time together. He'd never felt the urge to kiss her. She'd never really pushed toward that either.

A long silence hung in the room between them. Jason's phone chirped as he received an email, but he didn't dare look at it at the moment.

"You can get that if you want," Danielle said, looking back at him. Her eyes were glimmering like she was on the verge of tears.

"I think we should finish talking first," Jason said.

"Yeah."

This time, the room died into silence, with them staring right at each other, eyes searching for answers. He wanted answers, but he knew he couldn't find it with Danielle, as much as it pained him.

"I don't think we're right for each other, Danielle," Jason said.

"I know." Her voice nearly cracked.

"I like you. But there's too much history between us. It just doesn't work."

She nodded in agreement. After a long moment of looking out the window, she finally stood up from the couch again. "I guess I'll get my things, then."

"You don't have to leave right now."

She came up to him, getting up on her toes to give him a warm hug. "Jas, I don't want to waste my time. It's a long drive home, and I'll probably cry a lot, but I'd rather get it over with than sit here."

He hugged her back. What else could he do? "I'm sorry," he whispered.

"Nothing to be sorry about. It takes two to tango, my mom always said." She pulled back from him. Tears formed now, and she wiped them away. "Alright. I'll go pack my things."

Finally, she left the room, leaving Jason there. He slumped against the wall. This had been a painful moment, one he didn't want to deal with, but it was over.

In many ways, it was good. It gave him closure. He could move on with his life and…

…and what? Did this give him a path to a relationship with Rachel? He'd spent five days ignoring her, which hurt him too. He supposed he had to be honest with her, tell her what happened, but he knew that conversation wouldn't go over well.

Jason let out a deep breath, heading up the stairs. He'd have to face the music at some point; he might as well get it over with. If it were meant to be, she'd understand.

But on the other hand, maybe they didn't have anything either. Rachel lived across the country. He couldn't see her at the time or hold her like he could Danielle. Even though he and Danielle weren't exactly compatible, this was a harder ask for a relationship. Why was he thinking about her the minute Danielle left the room anyway?

Because deep down, if Jason had to admit it to himself, he was falling in love with Rachel. Why had he let his feelings for her get this far?

He shook his head and headed up the stairs to get to his laptop.

Space Adventures Online

#General

Dr. Donovan Conley: Hey what's going on everyone?

Ray Athan: Look who's showing his face.

Dr. Donovan Conley: What do you mean?

Aria Benoit: You've upset Veela.

Dr. Donovan Conley: What? I didn't mean to.

Aria Benoit: Shouldn't have ghosted her then.

Ray Athan: Don't know what you're thinking waltzing back in here like nothing's happened.

Lizyn (GM): Okay guys, settle down.

Dr. Donovan Conley: I didn't mean to cause any problems.

Ray Athan: Well it would be nice if you would tell us what's going on and not just disappear for a week .

Dr. Donovan Conley: Sorry, something came up in real life.

Aria Benoit: Couldn't send a message?

Lizyn (GM): Seriously. That's enough.

Ray Athan: Well he need to know he should think of other people.

Aria Benoit: I can't believe I agree with you for once, Ray.

Ray Athan: Eventually I charm everyone.

Aria Benoit: Don't push it.

Dr. Donovan Conley: I said I'm sorry. I'm guessing Veela's not around?

Ray Athan: Nah, she hasn't logged on in a couple of days either. You really upset her, bro.

Lizyn (GM): We don't need to harp on him, Ray.

Ray Athan: Yes we do, Lizyin.

[User Ray Athan has been placed on Time Out for 5 minutes.]

Aria Benoit: He had it coming.

Dr. Donovan Conley: I'm not offended, no need to do that.

Lizyn (GM): He needs to respect my authority in this chat. A time out will do him good.

Dr. Donovan Conley: Guessing there's no play tonight?

Aria Benoit: We seem to be in a pretty important spot in the scene. You might want to go back and read the logs.

Lizyn (GM): Yeah, we'll wait for Veela.

Dr. Donovan Conley: Well if you see her, tell her I didn't mean to upset her. Hopefully everything settles down again here and we can get back to normal.

Aria Benoit: Once you cross certain lines…

Dr. Donovan Conley: What's that supposed to mean?

Aria Benoit: Never mind.

Ray Athan: Woo! My five minutes are up. I'm a FREE MAN!

Aria Benoit: Boot him again, Liz.

Lizyn (GM): I don't think we can train the obnoxious out of his personality.

#DM-Veela

Dr. Donovan Conley: Hey Rachel. The chat folk say you're upset with me. I'm really sorry I haven't been around the last few days. Something came up. I hope you're okay. I enjoyed meeting you in Nashville and spending time with you. Hope we can still talk.

Rachel

Rachel opened the door to find a handsome man, nearly six feet tall, with black hair, brown eyes, chic glasses on, and a winning smile. He had a polo shirt on, teal blue, along with some khaki slacks. He stood like he owned the place.

"You must be Rachel?" the man asked.

"Uh, yeah," Rachel said. Her shoulders tensed. Who was this guy, and why was he standing here? Moreover, how did he know who she was?

Her father approached her, placing a firm hand on her shoulder, nearly making her jump.

"Ah, Rachel, this is Brett," her father said.

Brett raised a hand to wave at her.

She wanted to squirm out of her place at the door between the two men, but she was trapped for the time being. So why were both of them acting so strange?

"I invited Brett here," her father said, stepping to the side and extending his hand to shake the younger man's. "I met him at a church potluck a few months ago, and he's a good man. He's an insurance auditor with a stable job and a good situation. Since you've talked about how alone you've been in Nashville, I thought you might like to meet someone."

"Dad…"

Brett took her father's hand. "He's told me a lot about you."

Once the handshake was complete, her father stepped back. "It's no problem, Rachel. Just looking out for my baby girl. Why don't you two go out and get to know each other some?"

She stood there like a deer in headlights. Her father had set her up without talking to her first. Everything in her made her want to ball her fist and smack her dad right in the arm. But she wouldn't act so embarrassing. Not with someone standing here. He seemed like a nice enough guy that she didn't want to cause a scene.

Brett cleared his throat. "I was thinking I might be able to take you to Waffle Pantry for lunch here?"

Rachel wanted to run away, hide in her room, and slam the door like a teenager again. But she wasn't a teenager. She was an adult, and her father was right; she had been alone in Nashville. Her only good prospect had been Jason…

Jason.

Where had he gone? How could he show up in her life, be such a genuine man, a good writer—no, that didn't matter—a good person, and then disappear like this? Did he get cold feet? Did he simply not like her? Could she be that unlovable?

She had no reason to think this Brett would stick around if she was. What did she have to lose at this point, though?

"Okay," Rachel muttered, resigning to the blind date with the fellow. She glanced over her shoulder, and her father had already slunk away into the kitchen, leaving the two of them alone.

She turned back to Brett. His eyes lit up like a Christmas tree.

"Great!" He motioned toward the front yard. "Come with me."

Rachel made her way out of the door, closing it behind her before heading to the street. Brett drove a Lexus S.U.V., white with a black interior. It was pretty nice, a little too fancy for this neighborhood, but he said nothing about it. Her father had found someone who at least looked put together.

Brett didn't open the car door for her, hustling around to the other side. Rachel raised a brow at this lack of concern but accepted it. These were modern times, after all. They both hopped inside.

Her impromptu date started the engine as Rachel placed her seatbelt on. Once he had the car in drive, he did the unfathomable and put his hand on her thigh.

Rachel tensed. This was beyond aggressive; it was much like the men at the bar who tried to sneak a pinch or a pat where they shouldn't after getting drunk. Yet, Brett was stone-cold sober and making such a move! How could he?

If he noticed her aversion to it, he didn't say anything, looking forward and saying something Rachel lost within her thoughts. Jason would have never been so unchivalrous. Did the man think she was already his because he knew her father? He'd be in for a rude awakening.

"…and that's when I caught the biggest fish of my life. Impressive, isn't it?" Brett asked.

"Uh, sure," Rachel said, pushing her legs together and to the side to force his hand to fall away. This had been a bad idea. Why had she listened to her father at all?

Brett kept talking through the entire ride. It was like he couldn't turn his motormouth off. But she was trapped on a date, at least for the time being. Should she invent an excuse like she was feeling ill? No, it would be too obvious. She would have to wait it out.

After an eternity, they arrived at the Waffle Pantry, getting a seat fairly easily. It was only about three o'clock, and the crowds would come in again at dinner time.

A waitress sat them in the mostly vacant restaurant while Brett continued talking about himself, his travels, and his money. It was so exhausting to hear it all. It was no wonder how the man was single. She could also see why her father might like him. He came across as confident, indeed. Only a man with insane confidence could make such a move right away.

She couldn't get him touching her off of his mind. She'd been wearing jeans, so at least her leg hadn't been bare, but still. This was unbelievable. She ordered herself some fried chicken in the middle of being lectured. She wasn't particularly hungry, but she picked at it anyway to get away with just tuning him out and giving some "mm-hmm" s or "yeah's" during his never-ending speeches.

"I'm looking to be heading out to Nevada in the next few weeks. Fun trip," Brett said.

Rachel tuned back into the conversation when he mentioned the state. "Oh yeah?" Nevada was where Jason was at. "What are you doing there?"

"Going to Vegas. Party central, of course." He grinned.

Of course, it would be Las Vegas. Rachel wanted to go to Reno, though, somewhere completely different. One thing was for sure; her mind had been on Jason this entire conversation. She and Brett were not going to be compatible. As much as her father would be annoyed, she could tell him she didn't want to see the man again without remorse.

Daddy wouldn't like a man who grabbed her leg once she told him that story.

"You seem disappointed," Brett said.

"Ahh, yeah. I work in Nashville, and they say Nashville is the Vegas of the East. A lot of bachelorette parties is why. It's the last kind of place I'd want to go."

She thought she'd heard Brett mutter that he didn't want to take her anyway, but he returned to his stories. She'd picked her chicken clean to the bone even though she hadn't wanted to eat.

Idly, she wondered what Jason could be doing. Would he ever contact her again? She should have gotten his phone number or something off of the game. As it stood, she would have to wait for him to log back on. And who knew how soon that would be?

She hadn't logged onto Space Adventures Online much in the last few days. She found it hard to roleplay when she felt so hurt and abandoned. It was silly. She'd only met him a couple of times, but through the game, they'd built such a bigger connection than having merely gone on a couple of casual dates.

No, she wouldn't log on tonight. She still needed time to heal before she faced the others again. Ray especially would make fun of her with this situation going on. She had fallen too hard and fast and needed to get over Jason.

Rachel looked back up at Brett, He was handsome enough, but no, she wouldn't be getting over Jason with him.

Brett basked in her attention. "How about we find somewhere to get a drink after this? It's been such a nice afternoon getting to know you."

He hadn't asked her a question about herself the entire time. It took everything in her not to roll her eyes at him, but she would remain polite for her father's sake. He'd said

Brett was from church, after all. She'd let the guy down gently.

"Oh no, I don't like drinking. Besides, I'm here to spend time with my family. I think it's best to take me back home," Rachel said. It felt good to assert herself, even if it posed an awkward situation.

Brett seemed undeterred. "Next time, then." He picked up the check, paying for their meal. At least he'd done that much before sliding out of the booth. "Let's go."

Space Adventures Online

#DM-Ray-Athan

———

Dr. Donovan Conley: Hey you're not mad at me are you?

Ray Athan: Nah, just protecting Veela. She's a good woman and deserves some respect.

Dr. Donovan Conley: Good. I feel really bad about things.

Ray Athan: Well I hope she comes back.

Dr. Donovan Conley: Me too.

Ray Athan: You didn't get her number or anything?

Dr. Donovan Conley: No, I was dumb. Just communicated through the game server.

Ray Athan: Too bad.

Dr. Donovan Conley: I guess all I can do now is wait and hope she comes back.

Ray Athan: Yep. If she doesn't it'll kinda kill our plot too.

Dr. Donovan Conley: I'm not particularly worried about that right now.

Ray Athan: I am. Do you know how often a good storyline comes along? Not very.

Dr. Donovan Conley: I'm sure Lizyin would be thrilled to hear you say that.

Ray Athan: She knows. I am vocal about everything.

Dr. Donovan Conley: I've seen that. Ha!

Ray Athan: But yeah, Veela's a sensitive girl. What happened anyway?

Dr. Donovan Conley: My ex came back into my life the minute I got home from my trip. Showed up at my house.

Ray Athan: Wild.

Dr. Donovan Conley: When it rains it pours. I swear I had the hardest time finding anyone for a long time but as soon as I did it's like they can smell me becoming unavailable.

Ray Athan: Some sixth sense woman thing.

Dr. Donovan Conley: No doubt.

Ray Athan: Next time don't disappear. The timing was hard on Veela.

Dr. Donovan Conley: I know, I know. I don't want to hurt her. I really like her. Though is it really going to work, with me living halfway across the country from her?

Ray Athan: At this point, no. She's not here.

Dr. Donovan Conley: You know what I mean.

Ray Athan: I think you shouldn't worry about it. Have your fun, live for now. If it works, it works, if it doesn't, oh well.

Dr. Donovan Conley: Easy for you to say. I'm pretty into her. I don't want to have another ex situation.

Ray Athan: Then treat her right.

Dr. Donovan Conley: I hear you. Thanks for chatting.

Ray Athan: No problem. I'll be pissed at you if you screwed up my game for good, though.

Dr. Donovan Conley: Trust Lizyin to keep it going.

Ray Athan: I don't trust her for anything. You saw how she timed me out.

Dr. Donovan Conley: You deserved it.

Ray Athan: Bah!

———

#DM-Veela

———

Dr. Donovan Conley: Rachel, are you there?

Dr. Donovan Conley: I know I screwed up. I'm so sorry. I've been going through some stuff at home and I want to talk to you.

Dr. Donovan Conley: I hope you're doing okay.

15

Jason

She wasn't responding. If only the game had some way to check if there was a read receipt like so many of the other messenger apps. But it didn't. Jason fretted alone in his big house, which seemed empty since Danielle had left.

Not that he wanted Danielle back. Her appearance here had led to the problems he now faced. If she hadn't arrived the minute he'd gotten home from Nashville, he would have been talking to Rachel, playing Space Adventures Online, and not worrying about whether this woman in Nashville would ever speak to him again.

Did it make him stupid to care about her? They'd only met twice, even if they'd spent considerable time online writing together. This was a fresh relationship without any kind of commitment. He shouldn't feel this strongly about her. But when did feelings ever comply with how things should be?

The worst thing he could do would be to sit alone in this big house. Jason picked up his phone, thumbing through it. Who could he call, and where would he go to?

Out of his recent texts, he spotted Ryan. The other

financial planner had been to Nashville with him and heard about his diversions to see Rachel. He'd be the person with the most knowledge to at least understand the situation.

He thumbed a text on his phone. Hey Ryan, what are you up to?

About to hit the bars downtown, Ryan replied.

Got room for a wingman?

Always. Meet me at the Albatross at 7.

Thanks.

Jason locked his phone, putting it in his pocket. He was wearing a tracksuit with a t-shirt, not primed to go out and hit the town, but did it really matter? It wasn't like he was trolling for someone new; he wanted Rachel. This was just to talk. Besides, if he kept himself looking shabby, it would probably help Ryan to pick someone up.

He slipped on his sneakers and headed out the door.

THE ALBATROSS WAS an old bar situated in a small retail area where most of the shops had shut down by this time of the evening. It had a blue door out front, but the inside was filled with designs made of old oak, giving a rustic atmosphere to the place. The bar had dim lighting, accented by spotlighting on the pool tables and dart boards to provide the game players better vision.

Ryan sat at the bar, a frothy mug filled with a darker beer already in his hand. He chatted with the bartender as Jason approached.

"Doctors told me not to drink for six months, but here I am. Seems to be fine," Ryan said.

"You should really listen to them," Jason said, sliding onto the stool beside him.

"Jas!" Ryan released his mug and slapped Jason on the arm.

Jason braced himself with the bar. His friend hit a little harder than he realized. "This is your pickup spot? It doesn't look like a place where many women go."

"Not many, no, but when they come in here, I know they've got taste and are into gamers." Ryan tapped the side of his head with his index finger. "It's about quality, not quantity."

"It's good you know what you're looking for." Jason scanned the place, but there didn't seem to be a single female.

"So, what's going on with you?" Ryan asked. "You never want to come out bar hopping."

Jason shrugged. Ryan had him there. It wasn't his scene, and the last thing he wanted to do was talk to some drunk woman in a situation like this. "Alright, you caught me. I'm looking for advice."

"Advice?" Ryan took another swig of his beer. "On what? I usually charge for financial matters. I'll have to advise you that I'm not a C.P.A., and you should consult with one before—"

Jason ribbed him in the side. "Very funny."

"So what's it about?"

"A girl," Jason said sheepishly. His face turned hot. Why was this so embarrassing?

Ryan couldn't help but laugh. "You're coming to me for woman advice? You must be desperate. I remember you saying I do it all wrong, that picking up women in bars like this would never result in anything fruitful. Yet here you are."

"Yeah, yeah." Jason motioned for the bartender to bring him a drink. He was going to need one. "Vodka soda. Actually, make it a double."

"Must be a rough one." Ryan motioned to his mostly empty stein. "One more for me too." He turned toward Jason. "What's going on?"

Several more people started to fill the bar, which made Jason slightly uncomfortable recollecting his story. He scanned left and right before looking back at Ryan. There was nothing to be embarrassed about; people met online all the time, just not usually in roleplaying games involving spaceships.

It was far nerdier than he tended to be in any regard, but everyone had their quirks, didn't they?

"You remember how I disappeared a couple of times in Nashville?" Jason asked.

"Yeah. I wanted you to go out to the bars with us. Was the whole point of the trip."

"I thought it was the conference?"

Ryan waved him off. "You know what I mean."

Jason chuckled. "I guess I do. I met up with this girl I've been talking to online. We really hit it off. Connected in a way I haven't with anyone before."

"You hook up with her?"

"No!"

"Then, did you really connect?" Ryan smirked.

Their drinks arrived, and Ryan immediately switched their glasses to his new one and took a sip.

"Yes, we did," Jason said with some irritation. "But the problem is that Danielle was waiting for me at my house when I got home. I spent a few days with her, didn't get back online, and this girl hasn't replied since then."

"Ahh, you got ghosted."

"I think she thinks I ghosted her. What do I do?"

"Call her?"

Jason shook his head. "I didn't get her number. We communicated all through messaging."

"That was dumb of you."

"I realize that now." He couldn't help but laugh at himself.

Ryan put a hand on his shoulder. "Hey, if she doesn't message back. You live, you learn. You figured out what you like in a woman, right? So take it as a lesson and move forward if you don't hear from her. It's all you can do."

"It's not that simple," Jason said.

"Never is. But you can't dwell on what you can't control."

A dark-haired woman entered the bar, curvy with long black hair. Ryan immediately swiveled to face her direction. "On that note," he said, "I'm going to have to leave you for a bit."

Rachel

"Well, how'd it go?"

Rachel's dad was all smiles. He still thought this was a brilliant idea. But then, he felt that about all of his thoughts. Her mom sat with him at the kitchen table; both leaned forward, looking eagerly at her as she stood in the doorway to the room.

She shifted her weight t one foot, leaning against the door jamb.

"I can't believe you blindsided me like that," Rachel said. "I wasn't ready to go out with anyone, and the guy was a complete jerk."

Her father frowned. "I'm sorry to hear that."

"Yeah, well, you acted like I was some piece of property to just give out to this guy. You said you met him in church?" She crossed her arms over her chest.

"Yes. He's a good man, has a good job too, someone who might take care of you. It sounds like your job prospects haven't been working out lately, and— "

Rachel stamped her foot on the floor once, jarring her father from his speech. It was a childish move, but she didn't want to listen to him lecture her on this guy's virtues. "He's not a good guy, dad. He's a creep. The minute we got in the car, he acted like he owned me, tried to feel me up and everything. I don't know how you read that so wrong."

When her father contemplated something, he often had a crease above the ridge of his nose. Given the expression on his face, he didn't like what he was hearing. "I told you, I met him in church. He seemed like a nice enough man. He's got a good job, a head on his shoulders. You're telling me he didn't treat you with respect?"

"No, Dad. He didn't."

Rachel's mother clicked her tongue. "Well, I never have heard of such a thing. From a church-going man?"

"Just because someone goes to church doesn't make them a good Christian," her father said. "I thought I could read people better than that, though. I'm sorry, Rach."

She wanted to be angry at her father for the whole date, and she had more to say, but she felt the muscles in her face relax. She couldn't be angry with him. Even though she'd been blindsided by going out with this guy, her father meant the best for her, even if he didn't make the best decision. "Please, when you want to set me up with someone next time, can you ask me if I actually want to go out first? I don't like coming to the door and being shocked about what I'm going to do for the day."

Her father gave her a sheepish look. "Okay, I promise."

"Thanks, Dad." Rachel moved over to the couch and kissed him on the forehead. Then, she backed away once more. "I'm going to go simmer down in my room for a bit, okay?"

"Your mother and I will be right here if you want to hang out. Maybe we can play dominoes or something? A better date?" Her father smiled.

"Maybe later." Rachel turned and moved down the hallway to her room. Once inside, she shut the door behind her.

Her father meant well. She had to remember that. But still, her chest tightened. It made her feel miserable and like she was some property to be given away at his convenience. He hadn't meant this blind date to be such, but it still bothered Rachel.

She let herself fall back onto her bed, the small mattress where she'd spent her teenage years. The bed had five fluffy pillows on it, which took up a large portion of the mattress, along with a pink comforter with white flower patterns. The comforter was soft, as was the bed, and it brought Rachel warmth even with all of the irritation she'd dealt with this afternoon.

Perhaps it had been a mistake to come home. She knew what her parents wanted. They worried about her in Nashville, and with her floundering life working at a bar, they were right to do so. However, it wasn't what she wanted at the same time.

All she wanted was Jason. But what had happened to him? Maybe he had just as many problems as the guy she'd just gone on a blind date with. He'd ghosted her, after all.

It made her want to log back onto Space Adventures Online, but how could she now? She'd be so embarrassed talking to the others after she'd had her romantic ideas crushed by this guy. They probably wouldn't respect her anymore or want her to act as the captain character. It was something she couldn't face just yet.

Still, Rachel found herself migrating over to her laptop, which sat on the small desk across from her bed. She opened it and scanned her Instagram. Jenny, her coworker, looked to be out having a good time at the Caverns, a small concert venue a couple hours outside of

Nashville. She'd heard they had some good electronic dance music shows, but it was never Rachel's scene. However, judging from their poses, Jenny and her group seemed to be having fun.

Social media only made her feel worse. She was lonely, without any real prospects in life, with nothing going for her. She had to leave her parent's house, but she didn't want to return to her life either. So what options did she have?

Finally, she opened her email. Several spam emails cluttered her unread messages, but she noticed one from Ohtani Corporation. It was one of the dozens of companies she'd applied to after getting her degree, but they'd sent the application months ago.

She clicked on the email. The H.R. manager apologized for the delay but stated they had a hiring freeze while they evaluated their growth strategies. They were still looking and wanted to have her out for a personal interview if she'd be interested.

Scanning over the requirements, it wasn't her dream job by any means, but it was far better than the situation she had going now. This could be the first step up into something big, and she would get to use her degree. That would make her parents happy, at least.

Rachel smiled. This was the first good news in some time. Things were looking up. "Mom! Dad!" she shouted. "I have some good news."

#General

Ray Athan: Alright, so now both Veela and Donovan haven't logged on in a few days. What's the plan?

Lizyin (GM): We'll give it a few more days.

Aria Benoit: We can be patient. We owe Veela at least that.

Ray Athan: What about Don?

Aria Benoit: Meh.

Ray Athan: You just hate men.

Aria Benoit: Because men deserve it. Especially you.

Lizyin (GM): Play nice.

Aria Benoit: We're just messing around.

Lizyin(GM): Yes, but your messing around has had a history of turning into real bickering and I'm not in the mood.

Ray Athan: Well, what do you propose we do, GM?

Lizyin (GM): Why don't you and Aria casual RP and hang out for a little bit?

Ray Athan: You think she wants to play a romance?

Aria Benoit: In your dreams.

Ray Athan: I'd think we shouldn't risk having another Veela/Don blowup and disappearance. We can't really afford to lose more players right now.

Aria Benoit: Might be the first sane thing you've ever said. Have we seen Chandler? He hasn't been around much either.

Lt. Chandler: I've been lurking. I just don't do OOC discussion as much. I try to stick to the game. And there isn't a game at the moment.

Aria Benoit: Sometimes I think that's a better way to be. Ray actually has a good question though. What happens if our captain and medic are gone? Should we recruit from the other game servers?

Ray Athan: In the context of the game, I guess you're right about Don. Medics are nice but like we really need a captain or the game doesn't work.

Lizyin (GM): We're still going to give it a few more days. If they don't show back up I'll incapacitate their characters in game somehow so you can move the plot along. If another week or two goes by after that and they're not back, we'll have one of your take the captain role. Might be handy to put out feelers to the other chats too.

Lt. Chandler: I have some real life friends I might be able to convince to play.

Aria Benoit: That would be cool.

Lizyin (GM): I can always come back and play a full player character with Lizyin again. I don't like to do that and GM at the same time because it creates story conflicts, but you know how it goes.

Aria Benoit: I do. I've GMed games before. Which is why I'm not doing it now. I just want to play my character.

Lizyin (GM): I totally understand.

Ray Athan: Let's hope it doesn't come to that. I didn't get the impression from Donovan that he was going to be bailing the last time he DMed me, but he seemed a little sad. Might be good to try to get people's off-game contacts so we can know what's going on next time.

Lizyin (GM): Yeah, but people have a right to their anonymity too.

Ray Athan: True. I guess I wouldn't want you guys stalking me, especially Aria.

Aria Benoit: In your dreams, again.

Lt. Chandler: I would be up for casual play if you all want.

Aria Benoit: Alright. Play in the ship?

Lt. Chandler: Sure.

Ray Athan: Guess I'll come too.

16

Rachel

The sun had set by the time Rachel returned to her apartment. She fumbled with the keys, trying to rest her bags against the corridor wall, though one fell to the ground anyway. Once she had the correct key, she opened the door and picked up the bag, trying to hurry it through before it swung closed.

If she took this job, she wouldn't miss this place.

Nashville, however, she would have regrets about leaving. This city had been a home to her since college. And though she liked the Vanderbilt area far more than the less desirable area where she currently lived, it wasn't like she had to drive far to get to the places she loved to go.

The drive back from her parents hadn't been too bad either. Traffic cooperated with her the entire way. She'd left in the afternoon, and though it was nighttime now, she wouldn't be going to bed too late. There'd be work tomorrow, but her shift at the bar wouldn't start until the late afternoon either.

It gave her time to relax and unwind.

She left her bags at the door, too lazy to unpack for the

time being. Her room called to her—in particular, her bed. After a quick bathroom trip, she made it to her room and flopped down on the mattress.

Even though she had been sleeping on the mattress she'd grown up on for years, nothing felt like her current bed. It was strange how she remembered her room from her teenage years, but it still seemed like she slept in someone else's room. It had been too long, and her body had adjusted to the current one.

Overall, the trip was okay. She liked hanging out with her parents even if her dad had pulled the annoying maneuver of trying to set her up with that creep. She hadn't wanted that at all, especially not after having experienced Jason. Even though they'd only met a couple of times, they'd bonded in a way she hadn't in years. Or at least, so she had thought.

But then he'd disappeared from the game. Should she even worry about it now?

She had to. The prospect of a new job loomed over her, and she wanted to get her life situated, especially if she had to move.

Even though it meant uprooting herself and quite a lifestyle change, Rachel knew she would accept the job. There would be so much for her to handle in the meantime. She didn't relish packing this apartment, even though her belongings were meager. Her father would help her, probably even pay for movers, God bless him.

But she'd have to break the news to others in Nashville.

She'd first have to tell Jenny, but she didn't feel like calling her friend now. She'd wait until tomorrow. Maybe they'd hang out on a break. Chris at the bar would be the next to know.

Rachel let out a deep exhale. The stress had already gotten to her, even without her formally accepting the position. She'd sent an email telling the H.R. manager she'd think about it, but she'd mostly made up her mind.

Or had she? Why hadn't she just agreed? This was the international relations position at a company she'd always dreamed of going to, getting out of waitressing at a bar. But part of her was afraid to move. She'd be even further from her parents and wouldn't know anyone.

She shook her head. There was still time to think about it. She could decline later if it seemed too much of a move or accept and simply back out. Until she left her job at the bar, she had all the possibilities at her fingertips.

Those fingertips were itching to type and play Space Adventures Online. It'd been so long since she'd last played they'd probably be mad at her for dropping the current plot line. It seemed like the whole ordeal with the orb was also about to wrap up.

Rachel grimaced. Facing her fellow role-players seemed like a daunting task as well, even though it was all over text, so she wouldn't really have to face them. She could imagine the crap Ray would give her and then the disappointment she'd face from Chandler and Aria.

Oh well, she would have to do it sooner rather than later, wouldn't she?

She sat back up on her bed. Her laptop was still in her bag by the door, which she hadn't wanted to unpack at the time. Now it seemed like a lot of work just to walk over there. It was amazing how much travel took out of a person.

Begrudgingly, Rachel got up and dragged her feet back to the door. She opened her bag, clothes, and beauty products falling out of the stuffed suitcase. The laptop would be in there, buried inside her clothes. She eventually found it and pulled it out.

She should also get the chord, but it had enough power

for the time being. She could always get the charger after the low battery warning. It made her chuckle to think about how lazy she had become this evening.

Despite her lack of energy, she made it back to her room and sat down at her desk. She flipped the laptop open, and face recognition unlocked the computer. A browser was already open, allowing her to type in the URL for Space Adventures Online easily enough.

Fear swelled inside of her. What if her friends were angrier with her than she'd thought they'd be? It could be possible they wouldn't welcome her. She might have ruined the game by taking so long to come back.

Worse, what if Jason was back? How would she approach him? Her heart pounded at the thought, even though it was irrational. He was gone by this point, wasn't he?

With him, it made the prospect of the job all the scarier. But she'd deal with everything one step at a time. For now, she logged into her account.

A flurry of direct messages popped on her screen, overwhelming the general chat. Too many people had wanted to check on her since she'd left. It made sense. She saw Aria, Chandler, Lizyiin even Ray. How nice of him. But below all the messages, she spotted one from Donovan —Jason.

A lump grew in her throat. Should she look at it? Had she been too quick to give up on him after he'd met her in Nashville? No. He'd left her hanging. It was on him.

Thoughts raced through her mind, scenarios where he might have been in the hospital, unable to log in, or worse. She sucked in her bottom lip and then clicked on the message to read it.

Space Adventures Online

#DM-Dr.-Donovan-Conley

Veela: Something came up? That's all you can say to me? Why don't you tell me the truth?

#General

Veela: Hey, guys. I'm sorry I disappeared for a few days. I have DMs from all of you going to try to respond but I'm pretty sure they all say the same things. I went to my parents house for a bit, didn't really have a way to get back online. I hope you'll forgive me.

Aria Benoit: Veela! You're back! *Hugs!!!!!*

Lt. Chandler: Glad to see you here, captain. Can't wait to play again.

Veela: Thanks for the warm welcome. I feel bad.

Aria Benoit: Real life comes first. I'm sure Ray would say something snarky but he's probably asleep right now.

Veela :Did you progress the plot at all while I was out?

Lt. Chandler: Nah. With you gone, Lizyin thought it'd be best to wait.

Veela: Ugh. I'm double sorry. Didn't meant to hold up your game. I know how frustrating that can be.

Lt. Chandler: No worries. We can get back to it as soon as we get a time to all be online.

Veela: I'm excited to get things rolling. :)

#DM-Aria-Benoit

Aria Benoit: Welcome back!

Veela: Thanks so much.

#DM-Ray-Athan

Veela: Hey Ray. Wasn't feeling myself for a bit but I'm back.

#DM-Lizyin(GM)

Veela: Ready to get back going. Sorry for the delay!

#General

Veela: There. Caught up on DMs. Only person who didn't send me anything is Chandler.

Aria Benoit: Couldn't check on the captain?

Lt. Chandler: I try to stay out of the out of character business. You know me.

Veela: I do. I appreciate your commitment to keeping everything separated. Probably smarter to keep real life out of this.

Aria Benoit: Maybe. Sorry Veela.

Veela: It's okay. Gonna go back through the old logs and try to remember where we're at. Let's save the universe from this orb. :).

Lt. Chandler: Sounds good.

#DM-Dr.-Donovan-Conley

Dr. Donovan Conley: Whoa. You're back. Hey…and, yeah I guess that sounds pretty lame.

Veela: It does.
Dr. Donovan Conley: I didn't mean to ghost you.
Veela: Well, you did.
Dr. Donovan Conley: Yeah.
Veela: It sucked.
Dr. Donovan Conley: I'm really really sorry. How can I make it up to you?
Veela: I don't know. I don't feel like I can trust you much right now.
Dr. Donovan Conley: Fair. But I want to rebuild that. Do you think we can talk on the phone?
Veela: Let me think about it.
Dr. Donovan Conley: Take as long as you need.

#General

Dr. Donovan Conley: Hey guys.
Aria Benoit: Hey Don. Veela's back.
Dr. Donovan Conley: I see that. I hope we can play and everything's cool.
Aria Benoit: Me too.

#DM-Dr.-Donovan-Conley

Veela: Alright, I've thought about it. I have something I really need to tell you too. But you need to go first. Tell me the truth — the whole truth, you understand?

Dr. Donovan Conley: And nothing but the truth, so help me God.

Veela: Here's my number.

Jason

Jason stared at his screen for a moment longer. He had her phone number staring right back at him. It'd been easy to meet up with Rachel before, a quick trip to Nashville, no commitment, no expectations, but this had permanency to it. If he called her on her real-life number, it meant something more, didn't it?

He'd already thought they had a great time meeting, to the point where he'd gone out with her twice. And they'd kissed. What a kiss it had been. Her soft lips were still imprinted into his memory, etched there in a way that wouldn't fade away.

Her text tone seemed angry with him, however. At least disappointed. Would he be able to deal with her being upset with him? He remembered how Danielle would harp on him in their prior relationship. But he'd met Rachel. She didn't seem to have those kinds of proclivities.

There would only be one way to determine how this would go and what she wanted. She'd hinted that there was an important reason for them to talk, but what could it be? Would he have to apologize more for ghosting her after their brief encounter? He wanted everything to go back to how it was before, during the lead-up to their meeting, to where they were just happy to type with one another—and flirt.

It had been so exhilarating then, but now, he would be so upset if this went wrong. He didn't want to risk getting attached to her if she would blow him off or lecture him on how he wasn't the kind of guy she wanted.

If she genuinely were going to do that, though, she wouldn't be giving him her number. She'd do it in text and then block him, right? Probably get him banned from the game. She had a lot more clout with their online group than he did. If he made her uncomfortable, there'd be no way they'd allow him to stay.

Jason picked up his phone and typed in the numbers. It took him a few moments of staring at it to muster up the courage to hit the call button. Why should he be scared, anyway? They had a connection, and it would be easy to establish it again in theory.

The phone rang one, two, then three times. Afterward, a soft voice answered.

"Hey Jason," Rachel said.

He was caught off guard at how casually she said his name. It short-circuited his thinking. He'd forgotten how pretty her voice was. "Hi," he managed to say.

"I'm not good at this, so maybe we just skip the small talk?" Rachel asked.

"Sounds good."

An awkward pause followed.

"So… what made you disappear like that after kissing me?"

Another awkward pause. This time Jason had to figure out what to say. He'd had time. He could have rehearsed something, knowing exactly where this conversation would be headed, but instead, he'd just stared at her number like an idiot. Should he be completely open with her? Would that scare Rachel off? If he lied, he had a feeling she'd know. The woman was too intuitive, too smart to handle any nonsense.

"Look," Jason said. "We barely know each other." He shook his head even though he knew she couldn't see it. "Sorry, this isn't a good way to start."

"Not really, no."

"Alright." He took a deep breath. "I had an ex who was very close to me. We were going to get married and everything. Honestly, I screwed up that situation, and I knew it. I'm not perfect, but I've tried to grow since then."

"You're not really selling me on how great you are," Rachel replied wryly.

"I'm not trying to. I'm just being honest. Maybe that's not the best way to be, but I figure I owe it to you. Anyway, she showed up at my house when I returned from Nashville. She was adamant about staying for a few days —she no longer lives nearby. We stayed together and talked, but there was no spark there anymore. It didn't work. But I couldn't come back online, talk to you, or do anything while that happened. It was a mistake. I should have just told her to get a hotel room and go home but with our history... I couldn't do it. I'm really sorry, Rachel."

Silence greeted him on the other end of the line.

"What we had in Nashville—have on the game and when we talk—it's special. I'm aware of that," Jason continued, trying not to sound distressed, but what could he do? "I realized the minute Danielle came back you were the one I wanted, but I had to see things through and get closure. I know it probably hurt you. I should have been more communicative, I don't know. This isn't really a romance movie way to start a relationship. God, I hope you'll forgive me."

The silence remained for a long moment, but then Rachel spoke quietly, "You know, this might not be the most romantic phone call ever, but I like that you're honest with me. I went on a date too in the interim here, not exactly the same conditions, but I realized quickly what I liked about you what other men didn't have."

"Yeah?" Jason asked, hopeful.

"You're earnest. And I hope you'll stay that way. No more hiding things from me, okay?" Rachel asked. "I don't want to start a relationship that way."

A tingling sensation fell over Jason's body. It implied they had a relationship starting. Which was more than he could have hoped for. He'd half expected her to get mad and hang up on him or at least take a few days to think about things. Could this really be going so well? He vowed to himself he would treat her better than any woman had ever been treated. He'd make it worth her while.

"Thank you for understanding," Jason said. "I promise I'll be an open book from here on out."

"You're welcome," Rachel said. "I like you, Jason."

"I like you too."

"Guess we won't be blowing up the Space Adventures Online game." Rachel chuckled.

"I'm sure Ray will be happy about that." Jason couldn't help but grin.

"And this may be all too soon, but there's a reason I wanted to call you beyond this. Well, it's tied into it. I wanted to see where we were at before I made a decision," Rachel said.

"Oh yeah?" What could she be talking about?

"I got a job opportunity. A real one. In my field. Not just some waitressing thing like I have now."

"That's great to hear," Jason said. "Where's it at?"

"That's just the thing. It'll be based out of Reno. Not exactly what I was hoping when I told you I wanted to live n Paris or London, but beggars can't be choosers. Your area's become quite a shipping hub for the west coast, and the company has an office there. I'll be traveling to Asia, putting my international relations to work, but I can move out there. I wanted to talk to you first, though, make sure you'd be okay with it—that we'd be okay."

Jason's heart pounded hard in his chest. He barely knew her, true. He'd met her only a couple of times and talked to her online. But he had a feeling with her like he had known her all of his life. She complimented him in a way no one else ever had.

"More than okay. When do you fly out to check out the company? I'll get champagne."

Space Adventures Online

#General

Vccla: Okay, is everyone here?

    Lt. Chandler: Reporting for duty.

    Ray Athan: Let's shoot some aliens!

    Aria Benoit: I'll be in engineering if you need me.

    Dr. Donovan Conley: Here.

    Lizyin (GM): Feels like forever. I actually had to go back and figure out what we were doing with the plot and come up with a new ending. I had planned some big reveal with Jorin, your original contact from Palmer Station who sent you on the quest, but it's been so long I forgot what my plan was with him. Sorry. :) I hope you like what I rewrote. Let's get this party started!

#DM-Veela

—

Veela: Thanks for the talk last night. I appreciate it.

Dr. Donovan Conley: I appreciate you.

Veela: So sappy, but I like it.

Dr. Donovan Conley: I like you. :)

Veela: You're going to make me spit out my Diet Coke laughing! Haha

Dr. Donovan Conley: I like making you— okay, okay I'll stop.

Veela: lol

Dr. Donovan Conley: Hey I mean it that I enjoy talking though. Can I call you again after we're done playing?

Veela: For sure. We'll gossip about the game and everyone.

Dr. Donovan Conley: Sounds good.

—

#Sunflower

—

Lizyin (GM): The group returned to the sunflower, the white space they had occupied before disappearing before their eyes.

Lt. Chandler: "We're back." He glanced around.

Aria Benoit: She realized she was with the rest of them and scurried down to engineering.

Dr. Donovan Conley: He had apparently been with them the whole time. The doctor kept a watchful eye to make sure no one was injured, but his eyes also drifted to Veela, unable to keep his eyes off of her.

Ray Athan: ((Ew, stop flirting!))

Veela: She returned, no longer with an orb in hand. Empty. The captain was pissed. "I can't believe we spent all this time and went all this way for nothing."

Ray Athan: "Hate to break it to you, but there's An Aryshan warship out there."

Lizyin (GM): As if on queue, the Aryshan ship pelted them with pulse fire. The ship rocked.

Veela: "Ray, take the helm and get us out of here as fast as you can. Chandler. Fire back."

Lt. Chandler: He fired the ship's pitiful weapons at the greater warship.

Lizyin (GM): It's not very effective.

Lt. Chandler: He cursed to himself.

Lizyin (GM): The Aryshan pulse weapons pounded the Sunflower with more than ten times the strength of the meager mercenary ship's weapons. It short circuited their weapons array as well as the engines, leaving them stranded and helpless.

Veela: She tapped her comm button on her chair. "Aria, get our engines back online stat!"

Aria Benoit: "Working on it."

Dr. Donovan Conley: He looked around the bridge but it seemed everyone was uninjured for now. The large warship loomed on the viewer, but what could he do but wait?

Lt. Chandler: "Weapons are down, captain."

Veela: "We're in trouble."

Lizyin (GM): The Aryshan ship hailed them.

Ray Athan: He tapped his console. "Incoming transmission."

Veela: "Give me audio."

Nirral (NPC): "Greetings humans. As you can see, you have been incapacitated. We are going to bring you in via grappling hook and set up a bridge between our two ships. You will allow us through the airlock without a fight or you'll all be killed. Is that clear?"

Veela: She didn't like it, but she also didn't see a choice. They couldn't fight a warship full of soldiers. They'd be slaughtered. "It's clear," she muttered.

Lizyin (GM): The transmission cut. And as Nirral said, the ship grappled them and extended a causeway between the two ships. Eventually it shook the ship when it hit, sealing and creating an atmosphere over the airlock. The door popped a few minutes later, Aryshan soldiers with weapons pouring in. They searched every nook and cranny of the ship.

Nirral (NPC): Eventually, Nirral himself came aboard, storming onto the bridge, holding a pulse pistol in hand and jamming it up against Veela's neck. "Where is it?"

Veela: "Where is what?"

Nirral (NPC): "The orb. Don't play dumb. I know you had it. You haven't stopped anywhere for port and we just saw your ship."

Veela: "I got rid of it."

Nirral (NPC): He smacked her across the face with the butt of his pistol.

Veela: She recoils to the side, blood dripping down her lip.

Dr. Donovan Conley: He rushed toward her.

Veela: She held a hand up to tell him to stand down. "I'm fine. Stay back."

Dr. Donovan Conley: He didn't like it, but with so many Aryshans around with weapons, he had to keep himself at bay.

Ray Athan: He wished he could do something as well, but stood watching.

Lt. Chandler: Chandler held his post near the ships weapons.

Aria Benoit: Meanwhile, Aria worked furiously in the guts of the ship on the engines until Aryshans would bother her.

Nirral (NPC): He motioned to a couple of his guards. "You keep searching and keep them under lock. We're going to bring our interrogators in." He stormed off the bridge and back to his ship.

Veela: ((How many guards are we dealing with?))

Lizyin (GM): ((4.))

Ray Athan: Ray looked at Chandler, trying to get the man's attention in hopes they could spring on their captors.

Lt. Chandler: Chandler nodded to his traveling companion.

Ray Athan: He stepped up from the piloting station and stumbled over the step to the second level consoles. When he tripped, he barreled into one of the Aryshans. "Oops, I lost my footing! Ahhhh!"

Lizyin (GM): The Aryshan lost his pulse pistol, and it served to distract the other three.

Veela: Veela grabbed the pulse pistol off the ground and raised it to fire on the next closest Aryshan.

Lt. Chandler: Chandler took on a third, smacking the Aryshan in the arm to try to make him lose his weapon.

Dr. Donovan Conley: While the Aryshan was distracted, he pulled a hypo from his medical bag and injected the fourth Aryshan with a sedative.

Lizyin (GM): One Aryshan tackled, another shot, another injected, but the fourth socked Chandler in the face with its super strength after losing his weapon.

Lt. Chandler: Chandler went reeling into a console, spinning and sliding to the floor, crumpled.

Veela: "Chandler!" Veela screamed. She fired her pulse pistol at the final Aryshan.

Lizyin (GM): The Aryshan was incapacitated.

Ray Athan: Ray kept wailing on the Aryshan he tackled until he'd be knocked out.

Lizyin (GM): And he collapsed.

Dr. Donovan Conley: He let out a deep breath. "Now what? We still are captured by this Nirral guy."

Veela: "I don't know. Those creatures took our only power with the orb and now we're trapped here."

Lizyin (GM): As if summoned by the talk, several Kraleen appeared in a beam of light. The light consumed the bridge. "We have conferred. We hear you, and we know you have toiled as we can see all through space and time. Our policy is non-interference, as you know, but we had already interfered enough by allowing the orb to be found by you. It has been returned to us and is in its rightful place. As a gesture of our gratitude we are moving your ship across space and into the area you call the Earth Solar System. We are also providing you with a gift for your efforts in returning the orb to us. We have darkmetal ore, native to our system, which is rare throughout the known worlds. It is a strong ore and worthwhile to scientists. Thank you for your assistance."

Veela: Veela watched as the ore appeared, confused as ever.

Lizyin (GM): The creatures disappeared as did the light, leaving the ore behind. The ship received a hail from Palmer Station. The Sunflower had been transported across star systems.

Ray Athan: "Looks like the government is wanting a piece of us already," he said, returning to the helm station.

Veela: "Prepare for dock. I hope this darkmetal ore is worth all of our time."

Lizyin (GM): It would be. They would receive four hundred thousand credits from the Jupiter Science Institute for their discovery, more than enough to upgrade their ships and live well for the next few months. Until the next adventure. /End Scene.

Epilogue

Rachel

Rachel stepped off the plane and into the tunnel connecting with the airport. Reno's airport was a little larger than she thought it would be, given how the city wasn't one she thought of as a lively location. Unfortunately, she couldn't take a direct flight out of Nashville, having to stop in Dallas, which gave her a layaway of about three hours in Texas—enough time to get bored but not to do much else.

Even still, excitement coursed through her body, her blood pumping faster than usual and giving her a light-headed sensation.

The plane was only about two-thirds full, and though Rachel sat toward the back, she entered the terminal fairly quickly. Part of her hoped she'd see Jason there. Still, with modern security measures, the kind of moments of stepping off of a plane and directly into a lover's arms would be impossible. She'd have to wait to get into the baggage claim.

After the crowd disbursed into the larger area, Rachel

followed the signs toward the exit, clutching her purse to the right side of her body.

She and Jason had talked a few times before her eventual flight out. Most of her belongings would be heading out in a truck with a moving company, which should arrive in a few days. However, she had some clothes and belongings she couldn't live without until then.

Both of them agreed she should stay in a hotel in the meantime. Even though they had gotten closer over these last few calls, she still didn't want to rush things by shacking up at his place.

With her apartment here and a stable job where she could afford to live decently for once, things were looking up—even without Jason. But Rachel still couldn't help but be excited about her new boyfriend.

She stopped walking. A family dodged to either side, the mother giving her dirty looks for halting in the middle of the walkway, but Rachel had other things on her mind.

Boyfriend. It was the first time she'd thought of him as such. They'd never discussed labeling their relationship one way or another, but it seemed an inevitability given how they talked and that she was moving to Reno.

But their lack of communication had already led to problems. She couldn't help but be nervous about how he had ghosted her when his ex came back into the picture before. Even though they'd gone over the situation, and he'd been so forthright since then, so caring and loving, everything she could ever want in a man…

She was spiraling into thoughts again. The airport buzzed around her, people ignoring the woman standing in the middle of everything and moving around her to either side. It was a big world, and not everything centered around her or her fears.

Rachel took a deep breath. She was nervous. Of

course. With a big move like this, how couldn't she be? But she'd spent enough time on the phone with Jason not to worry, and this was why they'd both agreed she should have her apartment and her own life to establish so that she wouldn't be too reliant on him from the get-go.

From what she'd seen of the video calls they'd done, though, he had a lovely house. So much better than she could afford on her salary, even with the upgrade in pay she'd be receiving from waitressing. But no, she couldn't let her thoughts drift into too much euphoria either. While it would be amazing to have a happily ever after, she would have to see how it went.

Her phone buzzed, bringing her back to reality.

Rachel pulled it out of her handbag, looking briefly at the lock screen. Jason's name appeared there, along with a brief message, I'm here.

Seeing the words made her arrival so much more real. Yes, she'd already been standing in the airport but was about to meet him in person. For some reason, it made her more nervous than the first time. There was so much more at stake now. But he wanted her here. He'd told her so.

"You're the perfect woman," Jason had said on their last phone call together.

The thought of it made her melt where she stood.

But she couldn't stand there in the middle of the terminal forever. She clutched her handbag's handle, even with the strap around her shoulder. It was all she carried on the plane, hating to drag around big carry-on bags. Why do that when one could pack everything into a bigger suitcase?

Rachel shuffled forward, her heart thundering inside of her chest. She moved to a set of stairs beside an escalator, where a security guard stood, making sure no one snuck up into the airport who hadn't already been on a plane.

Rachel gave the guard a friendly smile as she descended the stairs.

At the bottom, by the railing, stood a man with unmistakable brown hair and eyes that shone up at her. His smile told her everything she needed to know—he loved her and truly cared about her.

It took everything in her to avoid trampling the people in front of her to rush down the stairs and over to him. Still, she waited patiently for her opening, maneuvering around a person's roller bag before finally clearing an open path to him.

The world seemed to slow as it did in the movies. If possible, she became all the more lightheaded as she approached Jason. He held his arms outstretched for her, and she collided right into him, wrapping her arms around his neck. He wore a soft cinnamon-like cologne for her, and she took his scent in as she buried her face into his collar at his neck.

His arms squeezed around the small of her back, holding her tightly. She looked up at him, happy for once. This was where she was meant to be. All of her worries were for nothing. Jason would take care of her.

"Hi," Rachel said in a near whisper.

"Hi to you too," Jason said through his bright smile.

He leaned in toward her face and gave her a passionate kiss that lingered for a long time.

Space Adventures Online

#Mars-Olympus-Mons-Heights

Minister (NPC): "Do you, Donovan Conley, take Veela to be your lawfully wedded wife?"

Dr. Donovan Conley: He held his head high, proud. "I do."

Minister (NPC): "Do you, Veela, take Donovan Conley to be your lawfully wedded husband?"

Veela: She sideglanced at Don before responding. "I do."

Minister (NPC): "You may kiss the bride."

Dr. Donovan Conley: Donovan wrapped his arms around Veela, bringing her in tight to his body, feeling the back of the fabric of her wedding dress as he passionately kissed her.

Aria Benoit: She clapped for the happy couple.

Lt. Chandler: As did Chandler.

Ray Athan: He let out a whistle.

Lizyin (GM): Music began to play, holographic fireworks shone overhead and the beautiful view from Olympus Mons, overlooking the Mars colony, loomed in the distance. A pathway was set for the couple to get into their skycar and take off.

Dr. Donovan Conley: He took Veela's hand and walked back down the aisle with her, happy to be with the love of his life.

Veela: She couched Donovan's hand and moved with him, smiling at all of her friends .

Dr. Donovan Conley: The driver held the skycar door for them as they entered inside. They gave one last wave as a newlywed couple before disappearing inside. "I love you," Donovan whispered to Veela.

Veela: "I love you too." She kissed him as the door shut.

Lizyin (GM): The skycar drove off, leaving people to attend to themselves and have some refreshments at the party.

Aria Benoit: "They are one dorky couple, but they are really cute I have to admit," she said, standing and smoothing down her dress. The engineer felt uncomfortable in the feminine formal wear, but she played the part pretty well.

Ray Athan: Ray couldn't help but give her the once over as she stood. "They are. Hey, and if you aren't doing anything, maybe we could get some happy coupling on."

Aria Benoit: She rolled her eyes. "In your dreams."

Ray Athan: He made a puppy dog face. "How about a dance?"

Aria Benoit: She looked at him skeptically. "Okay. But this is an act of charity, you understand."

Ray Athan: He took her hand and led her to the dance floor. "I wouldn't dare to think anything else."

Lt. Chandler: The security officer hung by the refreshments, picking at some of the snacks and not consuming alcohol. He'd let the others have their fun.

Lizyin (GM): ((That's a wrap. Congrats to the married couple.))

Veela: ((Woo! Thank you for the scene, Lizyin.))

Dr. Donovan Conley: ((Yes. Thanks for everything. See you guys for the next game!))

Like The Aryshan Wars Universe?

Do you like the Aryshan Wars Universe presented in Space Adventures Online in this book? Read The Stars Entwined here! It's based on a real book series that our characters roleplayed!

And please don't forget to leave a review for The Roles We Play on Amazon!